BLADE'S LAST STAND

Something buzzed past Blade's right ear, and he automatically threw himself to the bank. He landed on his left side and rolled to a squatting posture, the stock of the M60 pressed against his thigh.

There was a hint of movement in a large tree thirty feet away.

Blade squeezed the trigger, the M60 thundering and bucking, the heavy slugs ripping into the foliage and sending leaves flying in all directions, the tracer rounds showing he was right on target.

A harsh shriek greeted the Warrior's volley, and an indistinct shape dropped from the tree into the undergrowth below. . . .

Don't miss
BLADE #1: FIRST STRIKE

BLADE
#2 OUTLANDS STRIKE

DAVID ROBBINS

LEISURE BOOKS   NEW YORK CITY

Dedicated to . . .
Judy, Joshua, and Shane.
To John and Tracey, for your confidence.
To Wally Marcellus, the truest of friends, who will
never forget our "Great Sasquatch Hunt."
And to Popeye, who taught me the value in spinach.

A LEISURE BOOK

June 1989

Published by

Dorchester Publishing Co., Inc.
276 Fifth Avenue
New York, NY 10001

PROLOGUE

Dear God!

He was going to crash!

The pilot experienced the chilling realization as he watched the bluish-black smoke pour from the sputtering turboshaft engine. He knew the engine would die at any second, and the prospect of his helicopter falling to the ground among . . . them . . . caused a prickly sensation to erupt all over his skin.

"What's happening, sir?" asked a familiar voice behind him, a voice strained by obvious tension.

The pilot glanced over his right shoulder.

Hertzog, the young crewman, was framed in the cockpit doorway. His angular features were pale, a stark contrast to his blue uniform. "It sounds like the bearings are shot all to hell!" he commented.

The pilot nodded grimly. Hertzog might be young, but he was the best damn copter man in the California Air Force. "This old war-horse has taken its last flight."

As if punctuating the pilot's remark, the Stallion suddenly lurched to the right, the turboshaft engine coughing.

"Damn!" the pilot fumed, struggling to maintain control.

Hertzog clutched the door frame for support, his knuckles white. "We're going down, aren't we?" he asked.

"Yes," the pilot confirmed.

"Down *there*?" Hertzog queried, emphasizing the last word with a touch of horror in his tone.

"Afraid so," the pilot stated.

"Any chance of missing the city?" Hertzog questioned hopefully.

"Doesn't look that way," the pilot replied forlornly.

"I won't let those . . . things . . . get me, Major!" Hertzog declared. "I won't!"

"They won't get us, son," the major assured his crewman. "If I can ditch the Stallion without sustaining too much damage, we'll

·

cut out and head for the river. There are a lot of trees along the bank. We should be able to lose them there."

"I hope so," Hertzog said.

"You'd better strap yourself in," the major directed. "This might be bumpy."

"Do you want me to bag a few before we hit?" Hertzog asked. "They might hold back and give us the time we need to reach cover."

The major reflected for a moment. A pair of .50-caliber machine guns were mounted on the Stallion. Just one would be sufficient to deter those creatures below, but the risk entailed was too great. "No," he responded. "You might hit some of the humans."

Hertzog frowned. "I'm way out of line saying this," he mentioned, "but I think you're making a big mistake."

"We can't endanger innocent lives," the major noted.

"How do we know they're innocent?" Hertzog countered.

"You saw those pikes," the major reminded the airman.

"What a way to end a mission!" Hertzog muttered.

"At least I got off a coded message to General Gallagher," the major said. "They'll know where to find us."

"Our bodies," Hertzog commented, then departed.

The major surveyed the landscape below, his keen brown eyes seeking a suitable landing site. He could feel perspiration on his forehead and soaking his brown hair under his helmet. If he could only set the big chopper down before the turboshaft crapped out on him! All he needed was a little time.

But there wasn't any to spare.

The engine abruptly belched a cloud of grimy smoke, shuddered, and died.

"Son of a bitch!" the major snapped angrily.

With a whining groan, the Stallion plummeted rapidly.

The major reached over and flicked a silver toggle switch on the instrument panel, activating the radio. "Little Red Riding Hood to the Big Bad Wolf," he announced, hoping his call was being monitored in Yreka. "Little Red Riding Hood to the Big Bad Wolf. Condition Red. Repeat. Condition Red. The Goose is crippled. Probable impact at Mother Hubbard's. Repeat. Mother Hubbard's. Goldilocks is in. The Pied Piper was correct. End of transmission."

There.

One last message, just in case his previous transmission had not been received.

For all the good it would do them!

The major was compelled to devote his total concentration to the task of aligning the angle of the helicopter's descent, but the Stallion seemed to be endowed with a mind of its own. He wanted to come down in a large clearing not far from the Rogue River, but the copter was heading toward a dense stand of trees between the clearing and the waterway.

"Come on, baby!" the major coaxed the craft. "Don't do this to me! Not after all we've been through!"

The Stallion's tail started to swing to the left.

"No!" the major cried, desperately striving to maintain some semblance of level flight.

The Stallion rocked violently, and then the helicopter was spiraling downward at a frightening rate.

"Brace yourself!" the major cried, wondering if Hertzog would be able to hear him above the rush of the wind and the grinding of the chopper.

The ground filled the cockpit window, the clearing and the trees beyond the clearing visible intermittently as the copter rotated.

"We're going to hit!" the major shouted for Hertzog's benefit, bracing himself for the collision.

With a terrific, resounding crash, the Stallion plowed into the trees, all twenty-three thousand pounds of her, striking with the force of a bomb, leveling the first trees she hit.

The major saw the front of the cockpit shatter in a shower of plexiglass and metal. Something seared his right shoulder. His body was jarred unmercifully, his spine lancing with torment.

Her momentum scarcely checked, the Stallion slammed into other trees, her fuselage absorbing the brunt of the concussion. Her frame cracked and buckled. The starboard side crumpled like a flimsy eggshell with a rending, grinding roar.

His body flouncing in his seat, the major felt his neck whip to the right. He accidentally bit his tongue. For a moment he was completely disoriented, awash in vertigo.

With a surprising swiftness all motion ceased. The Stallion became still.

The major's heart was pounding in his chest. He glanced at his right shoulder and discovered a six-inch metal shard imbedded in his flesh. The jagged fragment had torn through his uniform and pierced his shoulder, narrowly missing the bone. A ring of blood encircled the wound.

Damn his luck!

Grimacing in pain, the major used his left hand to unfasten the seat restraints. He rose, his legs wobbly, and took several seconds to catch his breath and regain his strength.

Where was his crewman?

"Hertzog?" the major called out. "Are you all right?"

There was no answer.

The major staggered to the doorway, noting the extent of the damage to the cockpit, amazed he was still alive. He stepped through the doorway into the main cabin, then froze, aghast.

Hertzog had not survived the crash. The airman was strapped in a seat on the starboard side of the helicopter, his torn and mangled form partially encased in a shroud of twisted metal and protruding tree limbs. One of the limbs had speared him through the neck, nearly decapitating him.

"Hertzog!" the major exclaimed weakly.

The exit door located on the forward starboard side of the cabin had been crumpled into an accordion shape and twisted to the rear, leaving a two-foot space and affording a glimpse of daylight and the boles of trees.

Somewhere in the distance arose the sound of shouting.

The major moved to the starboard exit door and peered outside. Not more than three feet below was the ground. He cast a last look at Hertzog, then hurriedly slid through the two-foot space and dropped to the weed-choked earth. His right shoulder was racked by an excruciating pang. He flinched, doubling over, wishing he could extract the metal shard and tend to his wound.

But they would find him if he delayed.

His lips compressed to preclude an involuntary cry, the major hastened away from the helicopter. He scanned the tops of the trees, taking his bearings according to the position of the sun. Due west was directly ahead.

More yelling was coming from the east.

The major jogged in the direction of the Rogue River. His left hand brushed the grips of his .45 automatic, a reassuring gesture. The automatic was secure in a black leather holster, its butt forward in the time-honored military fashion. Even with his right arm out of commission, he could draw and fire using his left hand with a fair degree of accuracy.

"This way!" a man bellowed perhaps 50 yards to the east.

They were closing on the downed chopper fast!

The major skirted a wide tree trunk and entered a stand of dense undergrowth.

"Over here!" someone else barked.

The major bent over at the waist to reduce his profile. His left hand scraped against a thorn bush, drawing blood across his knuckles. He reached a shallow depression and eased onto his knees, then drew the .45.

They weren't taking him without a fight!

That much was certain!

There was a hubbub, a commingling of indistinguishable utterances, in the vicinity of the Stallion.

The major stared to the west, trying to spy the river. How far did he have to go? he wondered.

A new element was added to the commotion near the chopper when a deep, flinty voice boomed above all the rest.

"Silence! All of you will return to your work stations immediately! Move your asses, you worthless rabble!"

What was happening?

Had one of those . . . things . . . arrived on the scene?

The major rose, keeping his body hunched over, and hiked westward. After a hundred yards the vegetation thinned out. He encountered piles of weeds and brush at regular ten-yard intervals. Someone was in the process of clearing the area near the river. He advanced cautiously, moving past a large oak.

And unexpectedly discovered one of the occupants of the city.

The major halted in midstride, leveling the automatic.

A short, stocky man dressed in tattered brown pants and a brown shirt was standing five feet off, a sickle clutched in his right hand, an expression of astonishment on his oval face.

"Don't move!" the major warned.

The man gazed at the pistol, his mouth widening in stupefaction. "You have a gun!" he blurted out.

"And I know how to use it," the major cautioned. "So keep your voice down!"

"But guns are strictly forbidden," the stocky man said. "The penalty for owning one is premature consumption."

"Premature consumption?" the major repeated quizzically.

The man in brown looked to the east. "I heard a crash."

"My helicopter went down," the major stated. "I need your help."

The man gaped at the major. "You're not from the Province! I knew it!"

"No, I'm not from around here," the major confirmed. "And I need your help!" he reiterated.

The stocky man shook his head. "I can't help you!"

"Why not?" the major demanded. "I won't hurt you."

"No," the man said fearfully. "You don't know what you're asking! The penalty for aiding illegal entrants is premature consumption."

"There you go again!" the major snapped, frustration engulfing him.

The stocky man closed his eyes. "Please! Get out of here! I don't want to talk to you! I don't even want to see you! Go!"

"I'll go if you'll answer one question," the major declared. "Are there any boats nearby?"

"Boats?" The man in brown opened his eyes.

"I know I'm close to the river," the major said. "I could use a boat."

"No!" the man said.

"Look, I don't want to cause you any trouble," the major assured him. "I have a fair idea of what's going on in this city. I saw a lot of people from the air, and I also saw a lot of the monstrosities obviously running this place. I want to get the hell out of here before one of those creatures shows up. Which is why I could use a boat. Is there one nearby?"

The stocky man shook his head vigorously. "I can't! I can't! The Reptiloids will report me!"

"The Reptiloids? Is that what those things are called?" the major asked.

The man closed his eyes again, his lower lip quivering. "I just can't! Can't! Can't!"

"Now listen, you—" the major began.

There was the retort of a breaking branch to the rear.

Startled, the major spun. His eyes narrowed at the sight of several dark forms moving through the undergrowth toward him.

They were not bothering to conceal their pursuit; they barged right through the thickest vegetation, tramping bushes and breaking any limbs in their path.

"The Reptiloids!" the stocky man wailed.

The major hesitated, debating whether to make a stand or flee. He decided discretion was the better part of valor and took off to the west.

"No!" the man in brown cried. "No!"

His right shoulder pulsing with pain, the major weaved a zigzag pattern toward the Rogue River, putting as many trees between himself and his pursuers as he could.

A terrified screech rent the woods behind him.

The trees abruptly ended at the rim of a gradually sloping bank. Twenty feet away was the gently flowing Rogue River.

Elated, the major dashed to the water's edge. He glanced to the left and right, seeking a boat.

There was one.

But it wasn't available for his use.

A sleek, red motorboat rumbled into life 40 yards to the north, alongside a small dock on the opposite bank. The craft surged from the dock and shot across the water, bearing down on the man in the blue uniform.

The major took one look at the three figures in the motorboat and turned, intending to evade capture by hiding in the trees. But his retreat was cut off.

Three more of the creatures were perched on the lip of the bank. One of them, the largest, poised between his two companions, hefted a gleaming silver pike, and smirked.

The major raised the pistol.

"Have a care, human!" the thing stated testily. "If you squeeze that trigger, you will be ripped to pieces. You can not hope to slay all of us."

The speeding motorboat was already halfway across the Rogue River.

"I'll get one or two of you," the major vowed.

"Perhaps," the creature said. "Perhaps not."

The motorboat's engine created a raucous din.

"Drop the weapon," the creature on the bank directed.

"I don't think so," the major rejoined, smirking. He kept his pistol trained on the large thing in the center. They hadn't tried anything yet, and he was confident he could hold them off long enough to reach the trees. His train of thought was distracted by the noise of the approaching motorboat. The thundering engine was making an earsplitting racket. If he didn't know better, he'd swear the boat was right behind him.

It was.

The major managed a solitary stride before he realized his mistake and started to turn.

The creature driving the motorboat had the craft at full throttle.

Taken unawares, the major was unable to avoid the boat's prow. He saw the thing at the wheel jerk the wheel to the left, and the motorboat angled sharply. The craft slewed up onto the bank, and he felt a tremendous blow in his midriff and on his legs. His body was hurled backwards, tumbling head over heels. Everything was a blur for a second, and then he slammed into a hard object, his left side bearing the brunt of the impact. The world swam before his eyes, a pinwheel of blues and greens and yellows and reds.

Was he dying?

Slowly, sluggishly, his senses returned. A hideous visage materialized above him. Sounding hollow and distant, the voice of the large creature penetrated his waning consciousness.

"Foolish human! We must teach you the error of your ways!"

The major flexed his lefthand, surprised to find his gun was gone.

"Rest easy, human," the creature said. "You won't die. Not now, anyhow. But it may be a different story after your audience with Reptilian."

Reptilian?

The major sank into oblivion.

PART ONE
OF MUTANTS AND MEN

CHAPTER ONE

The giant was immersed in reflection.

He stood on a grassy mound 20 yards to the south of the command bunker, his keen gray eyes surveying the bunker, his forehead furrowed, his hands clasped behind his broad back. The rising sun was just topping the eastern horizon and there was a slight chill to the early April air. But the giant seemed not to notice. His massive physique was clothed in a black leather vest, green fatigue pants, and black combat boots. Strapped around his lean waist were two Bowie knives, one in a sheath on each hip. He brushed at a comma of dark hair hanging above his eyebrows and sighed.

What was he accomplishing here?

Was all the aggravation worth the effort?

He frowned as he glanced at the structure to the left of the command post, a supply bunker.

Three months had elapsed.

Three whole months!

And what had the Force done to justify its existence?

The giant shifted his attention to the building to the right of the command post, a long concrete barracks housing the members of the Freedom Force. They would be rising soon, and would emerge and assume formation to receive their orders for the day.

What did he have to tell them?

Simply the same old thing.

Drills, drills, and more drills would be the order of the day. And he was sick to death of repetitive practice exercises, which was highly ironic. Three months ago he had worried about their inexperience in functioning as a unit. He had demanded more time to train them before leading them into the field. And now here he was, fervently wishing the Force would be sent on a mission. They had drilled until they could perform their duties with skilled precision, but after three months of practicing day after day, three months of being confined to the compound except for occasional trips into Los Angeles, the members of the Force were beginning to get on each other's nerves. There were animosities simmering below the surface, animosities which threatened to explode if the Force wasn't handed an assignment soon.

Real soon.

A lanky man stepped from the barracks and began walking toward the command post. He wore buckskins and a pair of 44 Magnum Hombre revolvers in matching dark leather holsters. His brown hair fell to his shoulders. He took a half-dozen paces, then spotted the giant on the mound. "Blade!" he shouted.

Blade raised his right hand to acknowledge the greeting. "Boone! What is it?"

Boone jogged up to the mound, his brown eyes alive with excitement. He stopped and stared up at the giant, who normally towered over his six-foot-three frame by seven inches, and now loomed larger because of the mound. "We just had a call," he said.

"Who from?" Blade inquired.

"General Gallagher," Boone answered. "He's on his way here from LA."

Blade's interest was aroused. "Did Gallagher say why he was coming?"

"No," Boone responded. "He just said it's important, and he would appreciate it if you stayed close to the command post. He doesn't want you out on a training exercise when he gets here."

Blade scratched his chin. "This could be what we're waiting for."

"An assignment?" Boone asked hopefully.

Blade shrugged. "Could be. I want you to have the others fall out within ten minutes."

"Will do," Boone promised, and began to turn.

"Any problems last night or this morning?" Blade queried.

Boone paused. "The usual," he said.

Blade pursed his lips. "Kraft again?"

"Yep," Boone stated. "He just isn't happy unless he's making other folks miserable."

"What happened this time?" Blade probed.

"Last night Kraft tangled with Grizzly," Boone revealed. "If you ask me, I think Kraft is trying to commit suicide. If he keeps messing with Grizzly, he'll succeed."

"Was it verbal or physical?" Blade questioned.

"Kraft started in on Grizzly," Boone said. "He was griping about Grizzly being in the barracks, as usual, and I reckon Grizzly just had enough. He lifted Kraft off the floor and threatened to gut him."

"What did Kraft do?"

Boone snickered. "The idiot laughed, like it was all a big joke. Grizzly let him go, but I don't know how long Grizzly can control his temper."

Blade sighed. "Anything else?"

"A few minutes ago Kraft and Sergeant Havoc had a minor disagreement. Havoc was using one of the sinks to shave. Kraft decided he wanted to use that particular sink and told Havoc to take a hike," Boone detailed.

"There are four sinks and four shower stalls in the east end of the barracks," Blade noted. "Why did Kraft want to use the one Havoc was using?"

"Beats me," Boone said. "Thunder was in the shower, but none of the other sinks were being used."

"How did Havoc react?" Blade inquired.

"I wasn't there to see the whole thing," Boone said. "By the time I got there it was almost over. Kraft was on his back on the floor, and Havoc was using the sink like nothing had happened. Thunder told me about the argument. He said Kraft took a swing at Havoc, and Havoc did one of those fancy karate moves of his with his legs. Kraft stormed out of the bathroom cursing a blue streak." He paused. "Do you want some advice?"

"I'm always open to suggestions," Blade said.

"Then get rid of Kraft," Boone advised. "He's a monumental pain in the butt. None of us get along well with him. If he stays in the Force, you're only inviting trouble."

"If I send Kraft back before his year is up," Blade mentioned, "I could antagonize the Clan."

"We don't need a bad apple in the bunch," Boone remarked. "Not when our lives are at stake."

"I'll see what I can do," Blade pledged.

Boone nodded and jogged toward the barracks.

Blade watched the Cavalryman disappear inside. He'd known Boone the longest of any of the Freedom Force members, and he had developed an abiding friendship with the gunman. He tended to rely on Boone's judgment, and he knew the Cavalryman was right once again; if something wasn't done about Kraft, the Freedom Force would be endangered by internal strife. If the members couldn't relate well personally, they certainly wouldn't be able to perform their missions as a tight-knit team.

The Freedom Force had been the brainchild of the Freedom Federation Council, and he mentally reviewed its brief history as he pondered a solution to Kraft's disruptive presence.

One hundred and five years after World War Three, the North American continent was in a shambles. Devastated by nuclear and chemical weaponry, the United States had ceased to exist. Instead, diverse factions now controlled portions of the country. In the east the Russians ruled a corridor between the Atlantic Ocean and the Mississippi River. Chicago was under the heel of oppressive technological autocrats known as the Technics. Houston was dominated by androids. And there were other malignant groups, each in its own way determined to subjugate everyone and everything under an iron rule.

Fortunately for the sake of humanity, a number of factions were devoted to preserving freedom, to fostering liberty and maintaining the positive aspects of prewar culture. Seven of these factions had formed into a protective association designated the Freedom Federation. The leaders of this Federation had decided to establish a strike force to deal with any and all threats to the existence of the Federation factions, and they had named this elite squad the Freedom Force. Each of the seven factions was required to send a volunteer to serve for a period of one year.

Initially seven men, including himself, had constituted the Force. One of those men had been killed on their last mission, and the Federation faction from which the man had volunteered, the Moles, had not yet sent a replacement. Blade speculated on a possible reason for the delay.

The Force members began emerging from the barracks bunker, one at a time. They formed into a straight line, their backs to the barracks, standing at attention, facing the mound.

Blade suspended his reverie and walked toward his unit. He scrutinized the line from right to left as he approached, musing on the individual volunteers, on their strengths and weaknesses.

First in line was Boone. A frontiersman, he hailed from the

Federation Faction called the Cavalry. The Dakota Territory was their home range. They were a hardy breed of superb horsemen and horse women who, rumor had it, were taught to ride before they could walk. Boone was one of the most universally respected Cavalrymen, and his reputation as a shootist was widespread.

The second man was a full-blooded Indian, a member of the Flathead Indian tribe. They controlled the former state of Montana, and they had sent an expert tracker and marksman as their representative on the Force. Thunder-Rolling-in-the-Mountain was his name, and he had long black hair falling past his wide shoulders and alert, dark eyes. He wore a fringed buckskin shirt and pants, and moccasins.

The third volunteer hailed from the Federation faction known as the Clan. They resided in northwestern Minnesota, not far from Blade's birthplace, the survivalist compound dubbed the Home. And the Clan had sent, in Blade's estimation, the worst candidate for a position on the Force. The perennial trouble-maker, Kraft, was a Clansman. At five-foot-nine he was hefty but muscular. His lengthy blond hair was slicked and shaped into projecting spikes. He was partial to black leather attire and also wore thin gold earrings. In his right-hand pocket on his studded leather jacket he carried a switchblade, a weapon he wielded with exceptional skill.

Fourth in line was Sergeant Havoc. As the best noncom in the California Army, he was all military. California was one of the few states to retain administrative integrity after the war. As a recent addition to the ranks of the Freedom Federation, and wanting to demonstrate its commitment and capability, the government of California had agreed to construct the special facility for the tactical force near Los Angeles and to place the state's military hardware at the disposal of the Force. In keeping with their commitment, a soldier with impeccable credentials was chosen as the California volunteer. Sergeant Havoc was a qualified marksman and weapons master, a professional trooper with black belts in karate and judo and a brown belt in aikido. Six feet tall, with two hundred pounds of muscle on his frame, he wore his black hair in a crew cut and possessed penetrating blue eyes. He typically wore combat boots, fatigue pants, and a green T-shirt.

At the west end of the line stood the volunteer from the

Civilized Zone. During the Third World War, the government of the U.S. had been virtually wiped out in a preemptive strike on Washington, D.C. A few administrators and bureaucrats had made their way to Denver, Colorado, and they established that city as the new capital. The area in the midwest they governed was designated the Civilized Zone. As the largest Federation faction, both geographically and numerically, the Civilized Zone included a unique minority among its citizenry: mutants.

Their volunteer was a mutant.

Grizzly was his name, and he was the result of genetic experiments conducted by a deranged scientist. Prior to the war, genetic engineering had been all the rage. Geneticists competed amongst themselves to see who would enjoy the distinction of producing a new species. The U.S. Patent Office had even granted patents to scientists desirous of developing higher or altered forms of animal life. Animals with augmented, manmade characteristics were propagated. The genetic tampering with lifeforms was touted as a major scientific breakthrough which would reap untold benign benefits for humankind. Inevitably, however, the process was applied to human beings for militaristic purposes. By deliberately combining human and animal traits, by editing the genetic instructions encoded in the chemical structure of molecules of DNA, the scientist responsible for Grizzly's creation had hoped to produce a perfect assassin.

He'd almost succeeded.

Like others of his ilk, Grizzly was a curious hybrid of human and bestial traits. He was five-feet-eight in height and endowed with a thick body rippling with layer upon layer of muscle. His shoulders and upper arms were especially dense. He was covered with a coat of short, light brown fur, and he wore a black loin-cloth. His face was decidedly bear-like, with a pointed chin, concave cheeks, elongated nostrils, a receding brow, deep dark eyes, and small circular ears. Thin lips rimmed a wide mouth, and when he smiled or growled, those lips curled back to reveal a set of tapered teeth.

Blade absently gazed at the mutant, pondering the three varieties of mutations so prevalent since the war. Grizzly, the product of genetic engineering, was representative of only one type of mutation. The other two groups had been unleashed on the environment by the nuclear and chemical weaponry employed during the global conflict.

One of the more common forms included those wild animals born with their genetic code deranged. The enormous amounts of radiation which had permeated the ecological chain had warped the transmission of hereditary traits. Animals were born deformed with extra limbs or heads, or their features might be displaced on their bodies. Humans were also affected, but to a lesser extent. A few instances had been recorded in which a human embryo was radically modified by parental contact with food or water or land contaminated by the tremendous radiation levels.

The third type of mutation was the deadliest of all. It was comprised of mutates, former mammals, reptiles, or amphibians infected by the chemical toxins utilized during World War Three—specifically, the regenerating chemical clouds. Once they were infected, they changed from an average example of their species into insane, pus-covered horrors. They existed for one purpose: to kill and kill again.

Blade reached a point about six feet in front of the volunteers, then stopped to address them. "Good morning," he stated.

"Good morning," Thunder responded.

"Morning," came from Boone.

"Morning, sir," Sergeant Havoc said.

Grizzly simply nodded.

Kraft didn't bother to respond. He yawned instead.

Blade glanced from one to the other. "As Boone may have told you, we are expecting a visit from General Gallagher—"

"Good!" Kraft interrupted. "Maybe we'll finally get us some action, dude."

"So we won't conduct training exercises this morning," Blade went on, ignoring the Clansman's comment for the moment. "I want all of you to tend to your gear. Check your backpacks, your rations, and your weapons. We must be ready to leave on a moment's notice."

"Why don't we cut out now?" Kraft interjected. "We could split for LA and cop a little fuzz tonight."

Blade slowly moved over to the Clansman. "In case you haven't heard, discipline is essential to a military operation."

"I know that, man," Kraft said.

Blade leaned down until his eyes were inches from Kraft's. "Then perhaps you can tell me why you see fit to flap your gums while I'm addressing the men?''

"Give me a break!" Kraft rejoined. "It's not like we're out in the field. Besides, I'm sick and tired of all this chickenshit military garbage!"

"You volunteered to serve for a year, just like the rest of us," Blade noted. "You should have expected to be in a military unit. You should have expected there would be discipline and regulations."

"I didn't know it would get this bad," Kraft complained.

"It could be worse," Blade mentioned.

"Yeah? Like how, dude?" Kraft queried belligerently.

Blade's right hand lashed out, gripping the front of Kraft's black leather shirt. Before Kraft could so much as blink, he was hoisted bodily a foot into the air.

"Let go of me!" the Clansman exclaimed, grasping at the giant's fingers.

Blade's eyes were steely gray pinpoints as he unceremoniously dumped the Clansman onto the ground.

Kraft landed on his buttocks, his face turning livid. He made a grab for the switchblade in his right pocket.

But Blade was faster.

The giant's right Bowie swept up and out, the glistening blade sweeping to within half an inch of Kraft's nose. "Don't even think it!" he warned.

Kraft blinked several times in succession, gawking at the Bowie. His right hand stopped next to his pocket.

"I want you to listen to me, and I want you to listen real good," Blade stated angrily. "I have taken all the crap from you I am going to take! If you don't start shaping up, right now, you can pack your suitcase and return to the Clan. I'll even send a messenger back with you, carrying my letter to your leader, Zahner. I'll explain the reason you were mustered out of the Force, and I'll ask Zahner to send a replacement, someone who doesn't have bricks for brains, someone who doesn't act like he has a stick shoved up his ass all the time. Do you read me, mister?"

Kraft didn't move.

"Do you understand me?" Blade said in a gravelly tone.

Kraft, reluctantly, nodded once.

Blade straightened. "You've been a source of dissension since the first day you arrived. Months ago you promised me you'd toe the line, but your word obviously is worthless. You're constantly causing trouble, picking fights, and insulting the others. You don't seem to know how to function as part of a team." He paused and sighed. "I've tried to make allowances for you, Kraft. I know you were once a gang member in the Twin Cities. Before you became part of the Clan, you were forced to live by your wits. You survived because you were faster and meaner than your enemies. But your gang life is a thing of the past, and gang ethics won't hack it here. Either you learn to cooperate, or you can take a hike."

Kraft was glaring at the giant.

"Anything you want to say?" Blade asked.

Kraft shook his head.

"Fine. Then go check on your gear," Blade ordered. He stepped back and replaced his right Bowie in its sheath.

Kraft slowly stood, his rage readily apparent.

"You can return to the Clan if you want," Blade stated. "The choice is yours."

"No," Kraft said.

"Think about it," Blade directed. "It might be best for everyone if you did leave."

Kraft spun and stalked off toward the barracks. He slammed the door as he entered.

"If you don't mind my saying so, sir," Sergeant Havoc said in his low voice, "I hope Kraft leaves. We don't need his kind on the Force."

"We'll let him decide if he stays or goes," Blade said.

"Why don't you just boot him out, sir?" Sergeant Havoc inquired. "You'd be doing all of us a favor. Kraft doesn't know what it means to be part of a military unit."

"Everyone deserves the benefit of the doubt," Blade remarked.

"A noble sentiment," Thunder commented.

"And noble sentiments are just dandy," Boone chimed in, "except for one thing."

Blade glanced at the Cavalryman. "What's that?"

"If you're not careful," Boone observed, "noble sentiments can get you killed."

CHAPTER TWO

Blade was seated in a metal folding chair at his desk in the command bunker when the general arrived.

He was ruminating on his life at the Home, the walled retreat constructed by a man named Kurt Carpenter shortly before World War Three. The descendants of Carpenter and his followers still resided at the Home, over a century since the war had ended. As the head of the Warrior class, the expert fighters responsible for the preservation of the Home, Blade had spent most of his adult life safeguarding the lives of others. His fame had spread beyond the confines of the Home over the years, as stories about his lethal prowess were circulated among the Freedom Federation factions. He'd had to overcome countless threats to the security of the Home, and because of his demonstrated competence the leaders of the Freedom Federation had asked him to assume his new post as head of the Force.

Sometimes, he wished he'd turned them down.

His life was much harder now. Being in charge of the Force was a totally different experience from leading the Warriors. The Warriors were all devoted to their craft, they were able to discharge their duties proficiently, and rarely had they given him any grief. But the Force members, on the other hand, were a never-ending source of disciplinary problems, as in the case of Kraft, or else their attitudes left a lot to be desired. Grizzly was a bigot; the mutant had once referred to humans as "scum." And even Boone's attitude was deficient. The frontiersman had volunteered for the Force at the request of the leader of the Cavalry, not because he wanted to volunteer. Boone was merely killing time until his enlistment was up.

Blade abruptly sat up straight in his chair, listening.

The sounds of footsteps pounded on the stairs leading from his open office door to the bunker entrance. A moment later an officer appeared in the doorway, a brown briefcase in his left hand.

"General Gallagher," Blade said, greeting him.

General Miles Gallagher nodded curtly and entered the office. Gallagher served as the personal liaison between the Force and the governor of California, Governor Melnick. And it was Melnick who relayed information pertaining to threats against the Federation from the leaders of the Federation factions.

"To what do I owe this honor?" Blade asked.

Gallagher walked to a chair in front of the desk and sat down. He was a bulldog of a man, stocky, with brown eyes and crew-cut brown hair. A dozen ribbons decorated his barrel chest. His eyes narrowed as he stared at the Warrior. "Are you making fun of me?"

"Would I do that?" Blade responded, smiling.

"You don't like me, do you?" General Gallagher demanded bluntly.

"I never said that," Blade said.

"You don't have to say it," Gallagher stated. "I can see it in your face."

"I have nothing against you personally," Blade divulged. "But I do somewhat resent the way you feel about the Force."

"At least I'm honest about the way I feel," Gallagher said. "I opposed the formation of the Force, and I still don't think it's a good idea. Oh sure, I know all of the Federation leaders believe we need a tactical squad which can respond immediately to any perceived danger. But California has been taking care of itself for over a hundred years. We can handle our own problems. Funding and equiping a measely squad of seven so-called specialists is a waste of valuable resources. What do we need your squad for when we have an Army, Navy, and Air Force of our own?"

"We've been all through this," Blade mentioned. "The Federation leaders wanted a mobile strike force capable of dealing with isolated trouble spots before they developed into full-fledged threats to the security of the Federation. You just said you don't like wasting valuable resources. Think of the savings in resource material we achieve by having the Force deal with problems before they grow to the point where an entire army might be needed to deal with the situation."

General Gallagher reflected for a few seconds. "I never thought of it that way."

"Give the Force time," Blade suggested. "We'll prove ourselves to your satisfaction."

"You did handle the Spider affair nicely," General Gallagher admitted grudgingly. "Although you lost one of your men."

Blade frowned. "You don't need to remind me."

"Any word on a replacement yet?" General Gallagher queried.

"No," Blade said. "We haven't heard a thing from the Moles. I don't have the slightest idea why they haven't sent someone."

General Gallagher, oddly enough, grinned. "Well, we can't have the Force go out on a mission undermanned. But we'll get to that in a moment." He opened the briefcase on his lap, the lid concealing the contents from Blade's view. "You may have the chance to prove yourselves at hand."

"What do you mean?" Blade inquired.

General Gallagher gazed at the Warrior. "What do you know about Oregon?"

"Not much," Blade said. "We studied geography extensively in our schooling classes at the Home. So I know Oregon was once a state, and it was located due north of California. But, so far as I know, Oregon did not survive the war intact. You were the one who told me that Portland sustained a direct nuclear strike."

Gallagher nodded. "According to our records Portland was completely destroyed. A few rural radio stations in Oregon, those outside the blast radius, reported their employees could see the mushroom cloud. For a decade or so after the war California received a steady influx of refugees from Oregon, but they eventually were reduced to a trickle. Oregon is now consisted part of the Outlands, the regions outside the control of the Freedom Federation or any other known group. The Outlands, as you well know, have reverted to barbaric, savage levels of existence. Anything goes."

"Don't I know it," Blade said.

"I'm bringing all of this up because the Federation leaders want the Force to go into what was once southwest Oregon," Gallagher explained.

Blade rested his elbows on his desk and folded his hands under his chin. As the head of the Force he could accept or reject any mission; he had wisely stipulated such a condition prior to accepting the post. "I'm all ears," he stated.

General Gallagher's expression became somber. "We have reason to believe a confederation of mutants may be forming in the Outlands with the express purpose of dominating the country, if not the world."

Blade tensed. "What?"

"That's right," Gallagher asserted. "Let me give you the facts. From time to time we would hear rumors—just rumors, mind you—from refugees crossing our northern border. Tales about a mutant, a tyrant who'd set himself up like a pretty king somewhere in southwestern Oregon. We also heard reports that this mutant was in league with other mutants in the Outlands, and they were planning to establish a mutant alliance dedicated to eradicating or conquering all humans."

"Didn't you investigate these rumors?" Blade asked.

"No," Gallagher said.

"Why not?"

"Put yourself in our shoes," General Gallagher responded. "We hear all kinds of rumors concerning the Outlands. Everyone who comes from the Outlands seeking sanctuary in California has a tale to tell. There's the one about a mysterious group of renegades with a functional nuclear weapon somewhere in Nevada. And the one about the aliens from another planet."

Blade did a double take.

General Gallagher snickered. "The alien yarn is one of my favorites. There have been about ten people who claimed they were abducted by aliens in a flying disk, transported to a secret base on some mountain, and subjected to a physical examination. Later they were released unharmed."

"Someone has been pulling your leg," Blade said.

"That's what I thought at first," Gallagher concurred. "But then I noticed something strange."

"Which was?"

"None of the people making these ridiculous claims knew one another," Gallagher said, his brow creased. "And they all came from different areas in the Outlands."

"Did they say why these aliens were supposedly abducting them?" Blade inquired out of curiosity.

"Yep. And here it gets even weirder," Gallagher stated. "All of these kooks claimed the aliens were abducting humans to monitor us, to keep tabs on our biological development. The aliens were particularly interested in the long-term effects of radiation on our species."

"Very weird," Blade agreed.

"So you can see why we didn't believe the rumor about the mutant in Oregon at first," General Gallagher said.

"Something changed your mind?" Blade questioned.

"Yes. About a month ago a man showed up at one of our northern outposts. He was on his last legs, suffering from several wounds and severe malnutrition. The lieutenant in charge of the outpost took the man to Yreka," Gallagher detailed.

Blade knew about Yreka. It was a town of six thousand located in north central California, approximately 20 miles from the northern border.

"This man died," General Gallagher said, "but not before he told us an incredible story. He claimed he'd been held captive by the same mutant we'd heard about previously. He said he'd been just one of thousands of enslaved humans. But he'd escaped and managed to reach California." Gallagher paused. "And that wasn't all he said. He also told us where we could find this mutant."

"Where?" Blade queried.

General Gallagher reached into his briefcase and removed a map. He extended his arm and handed it to the Warrior.

Blade noticed the map was folded into sections and the word OREGON was printed on the cover.

"Open it," General Gallagher said. "Look in the lower left corner."

Blade complied, discovering a circle had been drawn around one of the cities in red ink. He read the name aloud. "Grants Pass."

"That's right," General Gallagher said. "Grants Pass. At last we have a definite location."

"What did you do about it?" Blade asked.

"We decided to send in a reconnaissance chopper," General Gallagher replied. "Grants Pass is about thirty miles from our northern border as the crow flies. We figured it would be an easy job. In and out." Gallagher frowned and stared at the floor.

"Something went wrong?" Blade deduced.

General Gallagher nodded. "We outfitted an old Stallion helicopter with our most advanced photographic equipment. The camera they used could pick up a fly on your nose from twenty thousand feet. We used our facility in Yreka as the communications link."

"You were in touch with them the whole time?"

"No," Gallagher replied. "They were under orders to maintain radio silence unless an emergency arose." He paused. "An emergency arose. We believe they crashed in Grants Pass."

"What makes you say that?" Blade asked.

General Gallagher reached into the briefcase and withdrew a yellow sheet of paper. "Here. This is a transcript of the two transmissions the Stallion crew made before they went down. The messages are identical. I think Enright repeated his distress call to insure we received it."

"Enright?" Blade queried as he took the yellow sheet.

"Oh. Sorry. The Stallion carried a crew of two. We wanted the bird to be as light as possible. Major Enright was the pilot. An experienced chopper airman by the name of Hertzog was also on board," Gallagher said.

Blade was studying the yellow sheet. "None of this makes any sense. It's like a page out of a book of nursery rhymes. Little Red Riding Hood? Big Bad Wolf? Mother Hubbard's?"

"We arranged a code in case any transmission was intercepted," General Gallagher elucidated. "Little Red Riding Hood was the code name for Major Enright. Big Bad Wolf was mine."

"Does Condition Red stand for an emergency condition?" Blade questioned.

"Exactly. Do you see the part where Enright says the Goose is crippled?"

Blade nodded.

"The Goose was the code name for the Stallion," General Gallagher stated. "The next line is the critical one. Probable impact at Mother Hubbard's."

Insight dawned. Blade looked up. "Mother Hubbard's was your code name for Grants Pass?"

"That's right. So we know the chopper went down in Grants Pass," Gallagher said.

"What about the rest of this?" Blade inquired. "Goldilocks is in? The Pied Piper was correct?"

"Goldilocks was our code for mutant activity," Gallagher disclosed. "The Pied Piper was the name we gave the man who told us about Grants Pass."

"So Enright was confirming your informant's story," Blade noted.

"Yes," General Gallagher declared. "You see, there isn't just one mutant in Grants Pass. There may be hundreds. But one mutant is the brains behind the operation they have set up there."

Blade leaned back in his chair. "Why do you think the helicopter went down?"

"I wish I knew," Gallagher said. "The chopper could have been shot down. Or it could have malfunctioned. It was an old copter, but we checked and double-checked all the systems before we sent it up."

"Why did you use a helicopter?" Blade probed. "Why not use one of your planes or a jet?"

"Several reasons," General Gallagher said. "The jets move too damn fast to take high-resolution photographs while flying close to the ground. A jet at low altitude would have flown over Grants Pass in the blink of an eye. We could have used one to take a high-altitude run, but we wanted, if possible, visual confirmation by the crew. A plane would have been slower than a jet, but a plane can't hover for an extended period of surveillance."

"You could have used one of the Hurricanes," Blade mentioned, referring to the two exceptional aircraft the California military possessed. The Hurricanes were jets with vertical-takeoff-and-landing capability. The governor of California had graciously placed them at the disposal of the Force. When not required for a mission, the Hurricanes were utilized as a courier service between the Federation factions.

"We didn't want to disrupt their courier schedule," General Gallagher said. "Besides, a helicopter was ideal for our purpose. Because of California's size, being eight hundred miles from north to south and nearly four hundred from east to west, we've worked hard at keeping our planes, jets, and helicopters in serviceable condition. The Stallion we sent had been overhauled about three months ago."

"How long ago did it crash?" Blade queried.

"A week ago," Gallagher said. "We sent one of the Hurricanes to each of the Federation members with a report. The leaders have unanimously agreed on how they want to deal with this." He looked Blade in the eyes. "They want to send in the Force."

"How soon can we leave?"

CHAPTER THREE

The two Hurricanes were waiting on the pad.

Blade scrutinized the VTOLs for a moment, then glanced to his left at the hangar. He spotted General Gallagher and several other people near the hangar and angled toward them. As he strode across the northeast corner of the pad, he reflected on the expense the governor of California had invested in the construction of the Force headquarters.

Located northwest of Pyramid Lake, which was north of Los Angeles, the headquarters compound was surrounded by an electrified fence enclosing all 12 acres. The fence was patrolled by regular California Army troops and was crowned with barbed wire. Because the Hurricanes did not require a long runway, a concrete pad 50 yards square sufficed as their landing and takeoff space. The pad and the hangar were located in the southern section of the compound. In the central area were the three concrete bunkers: the supply bunker, the command post, and the barracks. To the north of the buildings the land was preserved in its natural state for training exercises. An asphalt road connected the headquarters facility to civilization, and entrance to the compound was afforded by a gate positioned in the center of the south fence.

Blade abruptly stopped.

A woman was with General Gallagher! A woman he recognized!

Damn!

Blade advanced slowly. He was dressed in his full battle gear: Around his waist were his prized Bowies; on his back was a backpack fashioned from a waterproof camouflage material, which contained his rations, an extra pair of fatigue pants, and a packet of plastic explosive, a timer, and a detonator; a canteen was affixed to his leather belt in the small of his back; and he sported a pair of Colt Stainless Steel Officers Model 45's in shoulder holsters, one under each arm. And instead of an M-16, he carried an M60E3 general-purpose machine gun in his left hand. Two ammo belts crisscrossed his chest.

General Gallagher gave a little wave of his right hand as the Warrior neared his group. "The Hurricanes are fueled and ready to go," he stated.

Blade halted four feet from the general. He glanced at the woman, who stood slightly to the general's left. "Why is she here?"

General Gallagher cleared his throat. "I need to talk to you about her. And these other two."

Blade stared at two men standing behind the general. They were both professional soldiers in camouflage fatigues and outfitted with their field gear. He gazed at the woman again. "We have nothing to discuss concerning her," he said crisply to Gallagher.

General Gallagher appeared to be uncomfortable over the awkward circumstances. "At least hear me out."

Blade's lips tightened. "We've already covered this. And you can forget it! Take her with you when you go."

The woman finally spoke up, anger in her voice. "I have a name, you know! Or have you forgotten it, Blade?"

Blade faced her. "I haven't forgotten, Athena."

Athena Morris had her hands on her hips, and her lovely features conveyed her extreme annoyance. She was athletic and slim, with fine brown hair down past her shoulders and brown eyes which projected an aura of inner confidence. Her high, prominent cheekbones and thin lips accented her inherent toughness. Like the two soldiers, she wore camouflage fatigues and had an M-16 slung over her left shoulder. "So you two have been talking about me behind my back?" she demanded.

"I've broached the subject a few times," General Gallagher admitted sheepishly.

"At least a dozen," Blade corrected the general. "And I've given him the same answer each time. No way!"

Athena studied the giant for a moment. "What do you have against the idea?"

"I don't have all day to list my reasons," Blade snapped.

General Gallagher looked at Athena Morris. "Give it up. We've lost. There's no way he will let you on the Force."

"You've got that right!" Blade confirmed.

"I think I have a right to know why," Athena stated.

Blade stared at her, his mind awash with vivid memories of their last association. Once, Athena Morris has been a journalist, a top reporter for the *Times*. Seven years before, she had taken a plane from LA heading for Yreka to cover a story on a destructive flood. The small plane had crashed, and Morris had found herself taken prisoner by a degenerate mutant known as the Spider. She'd later escaped, and volunteered to lead the Freedom Force to the Kingdom of the Spider hidden in the Marble Mountain Wilderness. After the mission had been completed, General Gallagher had proposed assigning her to the Force.

"We'll discuss this after I get back," Blade now told her. "The Force is about to leave on a mission."

"Why do you think I'm here?" Athena rejoined. "I'm going with you."

Blade glared at General Gallagher. "She's *what?*"

General Gallagher mustered a feeble grin. "I said it would be okay."

"You said?" Blade stepped up to the general. "*I'm* the head of the Force! I make all the decisions pertaining to missions and personnel. And I explicitly informed you three months ago that I do not want her on the Force!" He paused, shaking his head. "You really take the cake, you know that, General? You've tried every trick in the book to try and convince me to accept her. You claimed I would be doing Governor Melnick a favor, because Athena could write favorable press releases after each mission and bolster his image. You even conned me into letting her live in the barracks for a few weeks after we returned from the Spider assignment, claiming she needed to rest up from her harrowing ordeal. And now you bring her here just as we're about to take off on a dangerous mission, hoping I'll accept your crazy idea!"

General Gallagher shrugged. "I try my best."

"Forget it!" Blade barked.

"You still haven't told me why I can't go," Athena interjected. "Is it because you don't believe women can be competent fighters?"

"No," Blade said.

"I didn't think so," Athena stated. "General Gallagher has filled me in on the place you come from, the Home. Your people, the Family, select a number of skilled fighters to serve as defenders of the Home, as Warriors. Right?"

"That's right," Blade acknowledged sullenly.

"And some of these Warriors are women, right?" Athena pressed him.

"Currently there are three female Warriors," Blade said.

"So why are you being so damn obstinate over my joining the Force?" Athena asked.

"The Force is supposed to be an elite team composed of a volunteer from each Federation faction," Blade elaborated. "Seven members and that's it. We don't have room for someone else."

"You're conveniently forgetting a little fact," Athena mentioned. "The Force has been undermanned for three months, ever since Spader was killed. And the Moles haven't sent someone to replace him. So you do have an opening, if only on a temporary basis."

Blade looked into her eyes. "We don't need you on this mission."

"I could be an asset," Athena declared. "You know I can shoot as well as most men, and I can live off the land without complaining."

Blade scrutinized her for several seconds. "Tell me something. Why all this fuss? Why do you want to join the Force so badly?"

"I'll be honest with you," Athena said. "Joining the Force would be a tremendous boost to my career. I'd get the scoop on all of your missions. I could report everything firsthand. The papers and the other media fatheads would be eating out of my hand. And my reports would be great PR for the Force and Governor Melnick. General Gallagher has told me how he feels about the Force, and I know there are some other people who feel the same way. My stories could be just the thing to convince them the Force is essential, that Governor Melnick is right about the idea."

"Your reports would bolster Melnick's political career," Blade remarked.

"What's wrong with that?" Athena rejoined. "Haven't you ever heard the phrase 'You scratch my back and I'll scratch yours'? What harm can it do to help Governor Melnick? The original idea for the Force was his, after all."

"I don't see what harm it can do," Blade admitted. "But you still can't come on this mission. It promises to be extremely dangerous. We will need all of our combat skills to stay alive. And while you might be a good shot and can live off the land, you're not a seasoned soldier. You don't have any military training."

Athena Morris smiled triumphantly. "That's where you're wrong."

"What?"

Athena glanced at the general. "Tell him."

"She has spent the past two months in intensive training with our Ranger Corps. They're the best we have, Blade. And they've put her through the wringer. She passed all of her courses, everything from Survival Techniques to Clandestine Termination," General Gallagher divulged. "She wouldn't be a burden from a military aspect."

Blade pursed his lips. "My compliments. You two seem to have covered all the bases."

"Thank you," Athena stated, grinning.

"But I only want seven permanent members in the Force," Blade said. "The Force is designed to strike swiftly, to go in, accomplish the objective, and get out as quickly as possible if need be. Additional members would only reduce our effectiveness. Any strike force functions best when it is just big enough to get the job done. The more members you have, the greater the odds of something going wrong, of someone making a mistake and endangering everyone else. Seven permanent members is all I want and need."

Athena saw her opening. "Seven permanent members, yes. But what about temporary members? What about temporary additions to the Force?"

"Temporary?" Blade repeated quizzically.

"Sure," Athena said. "Like now, for instance. You're one person short. You could use another pair of hands."

"We *are* one short—" Blade began.

"There! See! Why don't you take me on this mission as a substitute for the missing Mole?" Athena urged.

"Athena has touched on an issue I wanted to bring up," General Gallagher commented. "You've trained your men well, and each of them has certain areas in which they excel. But it wouldn't hurt, I think, to take along a specialist from time to time. Let's face it. Some of your missions might require the talents of someone with an expertise your men don't have. Like this one to Grants Pass."

"This one?" Blade repeated doubtfully.

"There could be hundreds of mutants in Grants Pass," General Gallagher said. "You need some added insurance." He turned and indicated the two soldiers behind him. "These men are your insurance. They're both Rangers and they are experts at guerrilla tactics. I strongly suggest you take them with you."

"Why don't we just take the entire Army?" Blade muttered. He gazed at the Hurricanes. Each aircraft could transport five passengers. If he took the Rangers and Athena, counting himself there would be nine.

"The Hurricanes can carry all of you," General Gallagher said, as if he guessed the Warrior's train of thought.

"Come on! Say yes!" Athena prompted. "We can be useful. We won't get in your road."

Blade hesitated. General Gallagher and Athena had presented logical reasons for taking the Rangers and her. But he balked at having to be responsible for the lives of three more persons. He was the head of the Force; their lives, in the final analysis, were in his hands. He'd already lost one man on a mission, and he didn't want to lose anyone else. Every time he lost someone, even if they died because of a boneheaded blunder on their part, he felt a certain degree of guilt.

One of the Rangers, a tall, lean man with a square chin and a set of bushy brows, stepped forward and saluted Blade. "Sir! We would be honored if you would agree to take us with you. We have heard a lot about the Force." He grinned. "Some say you're almost as good as the Rangers."

Blade couldn't help but smile. "What's your name, trooper?"

"Lieutenant Clayboss, sir," the Ranger responded.

"And you?" Blade asked, swiveling his attention to the second soldier.

The other Ranger snapped a salute. "Sir! Sergeant Rivera."

"And you two have experience in guerrilla tactics?" Blade inquired.

"Yes, sir," Lieutenant Clayboss replied. "We put in five years along the southern border."

"The southern border?" Blade said.

"Sí," Sergeant Rivera answered. "There are many bandidos along the border between California and Mexico. Bands of them like to cross the border and prey on the Yanquis."

"Do you speak Spanish?" General Gallagher interjected, speaking to Blade.

"No," Blade said. "Some of the Family members do. I've wanted to learn a second language, but I can never seem to find the time to learn."

"Sergeant Rivera is bilingual," General Gallagher stated. "He could come in handy on this mission."

Blade stared from face to face, noting the eager expectancy on each one. He sighed, knowing he couldn't rightfully refuse them. "Okay," he said. "The three of you can come."

"Out of sight!" Athena Morris squealed in delight.

"But," Blade declared forcefully, "I want certain things understood right here and now. I am in command. When I give an order, it is to be obeyed instantly. I don't want anyone grand-standing behind my back."

"Sir," Lieutenant Clayboss said. "Rivera and I are Rangers. Any orders you give will be carried out or we'll die trying."

Sergeant Rivera nodded.

"Good," Blade said.

"And you know I would never dream of giving you a hard time," Athena mentioned, smirking.

"See that you don't," Blade advised.

"Here come your men," General Gallagher remarked.

Blade glanced over his right shoulder. Boone, Grizzly, Sergeant Havoc, Thunder, and Kraft were approaching across the northeast corner of the concrete pad.

Athena Morris beamed and ran toward them with her arms outstretched. "Grizzly!"

Grizzly came forward to meet her, grinning, a backpack on his back, an M-16 over his left shoulder. He reached out as they met, gripped her under the arms, and lifted her into the air, spinning in a circle. "Athena! What a surprise! Don't tell me you're coming on the mission, gorgeous?"

Athena nodded as he set her on her feet. "Yep. The Big Guy just gave the okay."

Blade gazed at the unlikely pair of friends. Grizzly had become attached to Athena during the Spider assignment. The mutant had saved her life, and she had become quite close to him after the Force had returned.

Sergeant Havoc was walking toward the Rangers with a big

smile on his face. "Clayboss! Rivera! Don't tell me I'll have to baby-sit you two yo-yos this time around!"

The two Rangers shook hands with Havoc warmly.

"You three know each other?" Blade queried.

"Yes, sir," Havoc answered. "We go back a long ways. We were in the same squad when I was in the Rangers years ago."

"You were a Ranger? I didn't know that?" Blade commented. "I was under the impression you were Regular Army."

"Sergeant Havoc has a broad military background," General Gallagher chimed in. "He started his career as Regular Army, then he transferred to the Rangers for four years. After that, he was assigned to Special Forces. And now he's in the Force."

"Special Forces? The Rangers? What's the difference?" Blade asked.

"They're both elite units," General Gallagher replied. "The Rangers specialize in guerrilla warfare and engage in more generalized military activities. The Special Forces are employed on special missions, like their name implies."

Blade surveyed the men, woman, and mutant. "All right. Let's get this show on the road. Boone, I want you, Thunder, and Kraft in Hurricane number one with me. Sergeant Havoc, take the Rangers, Athena, and Grizzly in the second Hurricane. I want us out of here in five minutes." He stalked toward the VTOLs.

Sergeant Havoc, Lieutenant Clayboss, and Sergeant Rivera headed for the second Hurricane.

"So tell me," Lieutenant Clayboss said. "Is this Blade as good as they say?"

Sergeant Havoc nodded. "Better. I've never met anyone like him."

"That says a lot, amigo, coming from you," Sergeant Rivera mentioned.

"What's the scoop on the others?" Lieutenant Clayboss inquired. "We've met Athena before. We even supervised part of her training. The lady has guts."

"That she does," Sergeant Havoc agreed. "As for the rest, they're a mixed bag. The Indian, Thunder, is a hell of a tracker. Boone, the guy in the buckskins, is one of the fastest people I've ever seen with a handgun."

"And the mutant?" Lieutenant Clayboss questioned.

"He's a moody cuss," Sergeant Havoc revealed. "Don't say

anything to rile him or you'll regret it. And watch those claws of his."

Sergeant Rivera peered at the mutant, at the mutant's hands. "Claws, amigo? All I see are fingers and nails, just like yours and mine, only covered with hair."

"Grizzly's claws are retractable," Sergeant Havoc detailed. "I don't understand everything about them, but I know he has a set of wicked claws on each hand. They're housed above his big knuckles, and there are tubes or sheaths of some kind just under the skin, extending from his knuckles to the inner edge of his fingernails. There's an opening covered by a small flap behind each nail. All Grizzly has to do is straighten his hand, make his fingers go rigid, and those claws pop out. He can make mincemeat out of anything with them."

"You've seen him in action?" Lieutenant Clayboss asked.

Sergeant Havoc nodded grimly. "He goes wild. I know I wouldn't like to take him on." He paused. "Blade did once, and he won."

"How's that, amigo?" Sergeant Riviera inquired.

"Blade took on all of us," Sergeant Havoc mentioned. "It was part of our training. He wanted to evaluate how good we were, so he took on each of us." He grinned at the memory. "And he whipped us."

"Blade beat you?" Lieutenant Clayboss asked in disbelief.

"He sure did," Havoc confirmed. "Like I said. I've never met anyone like him before. If all the Warriors where he comes from are like him, they must be the meanest bunch of sons of bitches on the planet."

Lieutenant Clayboss studied the giant's broad back. "This mission should be one I'll never forget."

"Just so we live through it, eh?" Sergeant Rivera said.

"With the three of us together, it's just like old times," Lieutenant Clayboss declared. "What can possibly go wrong?"

Although Havoc didn't respond, a silent answer arose unbidden in his mind, an answer based on the circumstances of the last assignment the Force had handled.

What could go wrong?

Everything.

CHAPTER FOUR

The two Hurricanes were twin streaks of gleaming light as they arced to the north, rending the California sky with their shattering roars.

Blade used the flight to think about his new post, his family, and his future.

At last the Force would see some action! He hoped the mission would work as an emotional catalyst for those under his command. The perils they faced might bring them closer together as a team. Confronting danger often had such an effect on people. In any event, this mission would be Kraft's last chance to redeem himself. Either the Clansman began owning up to his responsibilities, or Blade was going to boot him all the way back to Minnesota.

He thought of his family, of his wife and son. Jenny and Gabe were trying to adjust to the vast difference between life in LA and life at the Home. Living in Los Angeles was a nerve-racking experience for them. The pace of life was unbelievably hectic. Los Angeles had been spared from a nuclear hit during the war, and the life-style of its inhabitants had altered only slightly. Oh, there were far fewer luxuries, and even some of the necessities, like fuel, were rationed. But the citizens of LA all seemed to constantly be in such a great hurry. The metropolis bustled with activity 24 hours a day.

The residents of the Home, by contrast, led an almost idyllic existence. Less than 100 people lived in the 30-acre compound. Led by the Family's wiser Leader and guided by the prudent Elders, they continued to uphold the beliefs of Kurt Carpenter, the man they referred to as the Founder, and to realize his exalted ideals in their day-to-day life. The pace of life was as slow as the proverbial molasses.

Blade knew his beloved wife was not happy living in Los Angeles. She missed the simpler existence at the Home, and she was worried about the negative impact LA might have on young

Gabe. The children in the city were hardened at an early age. They were belligerent and inconsiderate, and they exhibited a startling disrespect for their seniors. Flaunting authority was a typical trait. None of these deplorable attributes had prevailed at the Home, and Blade could readily appreciate his wife's concerns.

A voice in his helmet intercom roused him from his thoughts. He was wearing an Air Force helmet similar to the pilot's.

"Are you awake back there, Blade?"

Blade grinned. The Hurricane was designed with the pilot seated at the forward end of the cockpit. Next came two seats for passengers, which Blade occupied on the right, Boone on the left. Behind them were two more seats, currently containing Thunder and Kraft. In the sole rear seat was their radio and their piled backpacks. "What's up, Laslo?"

Captain Peter Laslo was one of four pilots assigned to Hurricane duty. The quartet rotated their schedules to insure that at least two of them were always standing by to transport the Force on short notice. "I've been meaning to ask you," Laslo mentioned. "How is your wife taking to LA?"

What was he? A mind reader? Blade idly stared at the ground far below. "Jenny misses our Home. She may change her mind after we acquire some friends we can socialize with. And I haven't helped matters much because I haven't been spending much time with her and my son. I've been too busy training my unit."

"If you want my advice," Captain Laslo said, "you'd better get on the stick and make time to spend with her, or she might just decide to head back to the Home, with or without you."

"She wouldn't do that," Blade stated.

"You never know about women," Laslo offered. "I should know. I'm an expert. I've been married three times."

"Why so many?" Blade queried casually.

"The first two wanted a homebody," Laslo responded. "A military man makes a lousy homebody. Duty first, and all that."

Was that the real root of Jenny's unhappiness? Blade wondered. Was she upset mainly because of his prolonged absences?

"Say, Blade," Captain Laslo said. "General Gallagher gave us your destination, but he didn't tell us exactly where to drop you off. Do you want us to deposit you in Grants Pass or outside of the city?"

"Just a moment," Blade remarked. He reached into his right

front pocket and removed the map General Gallagher had provided. Where should the Force set down? Certainly not in the city. If Grants Pass was swarming with mutants, landing there would be suicide. He unfolded the map on his lap.

Nearly twenty thousand people had resided in Grants Pass prior to the war. Thousands more had lived in the town of Rogue River, five miles to the east. A number of major highways had passed through Grants Pass, including the primary north-south artery in western Oregon, Interstate Five. Would the highways still be in passable condition? He was doubtful. Vehicle traffic in the Outlands was practically nonexistent. Few automobiles or trucks were functional, and gas was a precious commodity.

What was this?

Blade leaned over the map, studying a section to the west of Grants Pass. "I think I've found it," he said.

"A place to drop you off?" Captain Laslo queried.

"Yes. According to this map, about eight miles west of the city is an area once known as the Siskiyou National Forest. No settlements or communities are listed. It's uninhabited wilderness. I think our best bet would be to find a clearing and land," Blade stated.

"How far into this Siskiyou National Forest do you want to go?" Laslo asked.

"The farther, the better," Blade replied. "We don't want anyone in Grants Pass to spot the Hurricanes. Why don't you swing to the northwest when we reach the Oregon border, then bank around and approach Grants Pass from the west. We should be able to avoid detection if we're dropped off about ten to twelve miles from the city."

"Ten to twelve miles it is then," Laslo stated. "After the drop, we'll fly to Yreka and wait to hear from you."

"Hopefully this mission won't take very long," Blade commented. "I'm looking forward to getting back to my wife and apologizing for being such a neglectful idiot."

"Don't sweat it," Captain Laslo advised. "This mission will be over before you know it," he asserted optimistically.

But, as subsequent events unfolded, he was proven wrong.
Very wrong.

They were seated in the pair of seats immediately to the rear of the pilot in the second Hurricane, conversing as they watched the clouds flash past.

"I don't know how much longer I can stick with it," he confided to her, the person he viewed as his one true friend.

"What's wrong?" Athena asked him. "You've never impressed me as the quitter type, Grizzly."

Grizzly lowered his voice so only she could hear. Neither of them wore helmets. "It's the same old story," he told her. "None of the others want me on the Force. Why should I stay where I'm not wanted?"

"I think you're exaggerating," Athena said.

"Am I?" Grizzly responded. "You haven't seen the look in Kraft's eyes when he stares at me. He hates me, Athena. I can feel his hatred in my bones. He's always pushing me, trying to cause trouble. Sooner or later he'll force me to gut him."

"I know Kraft doesn't like you," Athena acknowledged. "But he must have a reason."

"How much of a reason does a bigot need?" Grizzly retorted.

"If you don't mind my saying so," Athena observed, "you're a fine one to criticize Kraft. As I recall, you're on the bigoted side yourself. You don't think very highly of us humans." She paused. "I'm somewhat surprised we've become friends."

Grizzly's dark eyes studied her for a moment. "It's true I don't think much of humans. Look at what humans did to the planet! The chumps tried to destroy it, for crying out loud! They unleashed a nuclear Armageddon and came close to wiping themselves out. In the process, they've perverted nature by creating a horde of freaks like me. Most of the humans I've met are vain and arrogant."

"If you have such a low opinion of humans," Athena brought up, "how come you think so highly of me? Or are you just playing games with me? I thought we were friends."

Grizzly looked her in the eyes. "We are," he assured her in his low, raspy tone. "Never forget. I'm a half-breed. Part of me is animal and part is human. And the human part of me, I'll admit, craves companionship sometimes. I want to have friends, just like anybody else. You're my friend for two reasons. First, because of what happened in the Kingdom of the Spider. Second, because I can talk to you without sensing any fear or revulsion. You're the only human who relates to me as a person."

"Now I know you're exaggerating," Athena reiterated.

"Why do you say that?" Grizzly asked.

"Not all humans hate mutants simply because mutants are different," Athena noted. "Take Blade, for example. You might try opening up to him sometime. He doesn't hate you, and he sure as hell isn't scared of you. That man isn't scared of anything."

Grizzly stroked his chin thoughtfully. "I don't know what to make of Blade," he confessed. "He's the only human I know, other than you, who treats me like an equal. I don't understand what makes him tick. I know he's deeply religious, which confuses me even more. How can he be such a deadly sucker and still believe in God?" He shook his head. "I just don't get it."

"I asked him about that once," Athena divulged.

"What did he say?"

"Blade said the spiritual must protect themselves from the unspiritual, or something to that effect," Athena stated.

"I still don't get it," Grizzly said.

"What about the others?" Athena probed. "How are they treating you now? You've been working together for three months. Surely at least one of them could be considered a friend?"

"Nope," Grizzly responded. "Boone treats me decently, but I can't tell if it's all a front or if he's serious. Thunder is real reserved around me. I know he's on the superstitious side, and I suspect he sees me as some kind of bad omen. It's all a lot of Indian nonsense."

"What about Sergeant Havoc?" Athena inquired, lowering her voice to almost a whisper.

"Havoc keeps his feelings to himself," Grizzly answered. "I don't think he dislikes me, but I don't think he's crazy about having me on the Force either."

"Give them time," Athena suggested. "They'll come around."

"Who cares?" Grizzly rejoined. "I don't need them. I don't need anyone."

"Oh, really? I'll bear that in mind," Athena remarked.

Grizzly reached out and placed his right hand on her forearm. "I didn't mean that to come out the way it sounded."

Athena decided to change the subject. "General Gallagher briefed me on this mission. We could be biting off more than we can handle."

"Don't you worry," Grizzly said. "I'm not going to let

anything harm you."

"What if Gallagher is right? What if there are hundreds of mutants in Grants Pass?" Athena commented.

"I have nothing against mutants," Grizzly quipped.

Athena gazed at him for several seconds. "How do you feel about having to fight other mutants?"

"I learned a lesson during the Spider affair," Grizzly replied. "Some mutants can be as bad as humans. They're an insult to my species." He raised his right hand and wiggled his fingertips. "And I don't like being insulted."

"I've been meaning to ask you about those claws of yours," Athena mentioned.

"What about them?"

"When you lock your fingers, the claws pop out those holes behind your nails, right?"

"Yeah. So?" Grizzly responded.

"So do you have to keep your fingers straight when you're using your claws?" Athena inquired.

"Yep," Grizzly said. "If I relax my hand, the claws automatically retract. But when my fingers are rigid, they stay out. It's weird. I've never heard of anyone or anything with retractable claws just like mine."

"Neither have I," Athena declared.

"When we get to our destination," Grizzly advised, "stay close to me."

"I don't need a protector," Athena said. "I can take care of myself, thank you."

"I know that," Grizzly stated.

"Then why do you want me to stay close to you?" Athena wanted to know.

Grizzly grinned. "So you can keep an eye on me. You never know when I might need some protecting."

Athena laughed. "That'll be the day!"

The Hurricane began banking to the northwest.

PART TWO
OF MEN AND REPTILOIDS

CHAPTER FIVE

The Hurricanes rose vertically for several hundred feet, then hung motionless in the Hover Mode. Captain Laslo waved.

Blade returned the gesture.

With a rumble of their mighty engines, the Hurricanes shifted into horizontal flight and winged higher and higher, bearing to the south.

"We're on our own," Athena commented.

Blade turned. His team was waiting for their orders. They were strung out in a line in the middle of a huge field in the Siskiyou National Forest. By his estimation, they were 11 or 12 miles west of Grants Pass. Athena was first, then Grizzly, Boone, and Kraft. Thunder came after the Clansman, followed by Sergeant Havoc, Lieutenant Clayboss, and Sergeant Rivera. Kraft was carrying their radio.

"I'll take the point if you want," Boone offered.

"No," Boone said. "Grizzly, you take the point. Stay alert. Head due east, and try to stay within fifty yards of us."

Grizzly nodded and jogged to the east.

"The rest of you!" Blade declared. "Keep on your toes! We don't know what we'll find here. And Kraft, don't let anything happen to the radio."

The field radio was strapped to the Clansman's back alongside his backpack. Kraft, like the others, carried an M-16 and wore a pair of Colt automatics strapped around his waist. "Chill out, dude," he rejoined. "Nothing will happen to the squawk box."

"See that it doesn't," Blade cautioned. He glanced to the east.

Grizzly was fast approaching the treeline. The mutant and Boone had both declined the use of a pair of Colts, Boone because he preferred his Hombre revolvers at close range, Grizzly because he relied upon his claws for the "personal touch," as he put it.

"Move out!" Blade directed, heading after Grizzly.

The Force members followed on the heels of their leader, with the Rangers bringing up the rear.

Athena scrutinized the Warrior's machine gun. "Say, Blade. What's with the change in firepower? Did you get tired of using an M-16?"

"No," Blade said. "We might need some extra punch on this trip, so I brought this along."

"What is it?"

"It's an M60E3," Blade disclosed. "General Gallagher provided it. This gun will put out ten rounds a second, and it allows me the option of mixing armor-piercing, ball, and tracer rounds in the belt. The stopping power and range are both greater than the M-16."

"I noticed that ammo belt you have in there is dangling down to your ankles," Athena commented. "I hope you don't trip over your own feet."

"I'll try not to," Blade said, grinning.

The Force quickly crossed the field and reached the trees.

Blade held up his right hand, then twisted to face them. "From here on out there will be no talking." He looked at Athena. "And I do mean no talking. Watch for my hand signals. Let's go!" He moved into the dense forest, hoping the system of hand signs he had developed would serve them in good stead. Far ahead he spied Grizzly, waiting for them to get within a range of 50 yards.

After a few seconds the mutant melted into the wall of vegetation.

Blade led his team ever eastward, his senses primed, alert for an ambush. A prolific assortment of trees and shrubs furnished ample cover, screening the Force from observation. But the undergrowth could work against them as well by harboring an enemy force lying in wait. He wasn't about to take any chances.

Within a mile they came to a creek.

Grizzly was waiting on the bank, scanning the opposite side.

"Why did you stop?" Blade asked in a hushed tone as he neared the mutant. He held up his right fist, indicating the Force should halt.

Grizzly stared at the giant. "I wanted you to know."

"Know what?" Blade queried.

"I think we're being watched," Grizzly stated.

Blade surveyed the trees on the far bank. "I don't see anything."

"Neither do I," Grizzly affirmed.

"Then what makes you think we're being watched?" Blade questioned.

Grizzly frowned. "I'm not sure," he said uncertainly. "A feeling I have."

Blade was surprised by the mutant's vacillation. Grizzly's animal instincts were normally unerring, his eyesight and hearing were hyper-sharp, and his scenting ability was uncanny. "Have you seen any tracks?"

"Just wildlife," Grizzly replied.

"Have you heard anything out of the ordinary?" Blade inquired.

"Nothing," Grizzly responded. "I told you. I have a feeling."

"Well, we won't take your feeling lightly," Blade said. "Head out, but keep within ten yards. I don't want to lose eye contact."

Grizzly nodded, then promptly forded the creek.

Blade motioned for Athena to join him on the bank.

"What's up?" she asked, her M-16 cradled in her arms.

"You know some of the hand signals we use because you were with us on our last mission," Blade observed. "But I've developed a few more since then. I don't have the time to teach them all to you now, so when necessary I'll relay my instructions verbally." He paused. "We could have company. Pass it down the line. And whisper."

Athena nodded, then turned and walked to Boone.

Blade entered the creek, the water swirling up to his knees. He crossed quickly and posted himself on the bank to cover the others.

Athena waded into the water.

Blade felt a peculiar prickly sensation on the back of his neck and pivoted, examining the nearest vegetation.

Grizzly was right.

Someone . . . or something . . . was out there . . . somewhere.

Watching them.

Was it friend or foe?

Blade touched his finger to the trigger of the M60. What could possibly elude Grizzly's enhanced senses?

Athena reached the bank and stepped up to the Warrior's side.

Boone was starting into the creek.

Blade checked on Grizzly. The mutant was ten yards into the forest, watching them ford.

Boone crossed and Kraft gingerly stepped into the river.

A strange whistle sounded from the woods to the northeast.

And all hell broke loose.

Blade was turning in the direction of the whistle when Athena suddenly cried out.

"Kraft!" she yelled in alarm.

Blade spun.

Kraft was in midstream. He had dropped his M-16 and was clutching at a red object partially imbedded in his neck. His arms seemed sluggish and weak, and his eyelids quivered as he tottered to the right.

Thunder jumped into the creek, going to Kraft's aid.

Blade took a step into the water, planning to assist the Flathead.

The forest abruptly rocked to the blasting of automatic weapons as Sergeant Havoc, Lieutenant Clayboss, and Sergeant Rivera opened up from the west bank. They were standing near the creek, their M-16's trained on the vegetation on the east bank, firing into the trees.

Athena and Boone joined in.

Blade saw Thunder stiffen and twist. A bright red object had appeared on the Indian's left shoulder. He tried to grasp the thing, but his fingers went slack and he stumbled and almost fell.

Just then Kraft sprawled into the creek, on his back, his arms and legs spread-eagled, and began to drift downstream.

Something buzzed past Blade's right ear, and he automatically threw himself to the bank. He landed on his left side and rolled to a squatting posture, the stock of the M60 pressed against his stout thigh.

There was a hint of movement in a large tree 30 feet away.

Blade squeezed the trigger, the M60 thundering and bucking, the heavy slugs ripping into the foliage and sending leaves flying in all directions, the tracer rounds showing he was right on target.

A harsh shriek greeted the Warrior's volley, and an indistinct shape dropped from the tree into the undergrowth below.

Blade risked a hasty glance at the creek, and he was appalled to see Thunder and Kraft floating from view around a bend to the south. "Cover me!" he bellowed, and lunged to his feet.

The Force members continued to pour lead into the woods.

Blade raced along the bank after Kraft and Thunder. Kraft had been floating on his back, but Thunder had been face down, and

Blade was worried the Flathead would drown if he didn't reach them in time. He crashed through a bush bordering the creek, his legs pounding, and reached the bend within seconds.

And stopped cold, astonished.

Where were they?

Blade looked to the right and the left, perplexed. The creek ran straight for several hundred yards. There was no sign of the Flathead and the Clansman, but they couldn't possibly have covered the distance to the next curve in the brief span it had taken him to reach the bend.

Dear Spirit!

Where *were* they?

Blade advanced a few yards, scouring the terrain for some indication of their whereabouts, baffled.

How could they just disappear?

The underbrush grew right up to the creek here and there, but the vegetation was untrampled and still.

Damn!

Blade whirled and raced back to his companions.

Athena, Lieutenant Clayboss, and Sergeant Rivera were still firing into the trees. Boone and Sergeant Havoc had ceased and were scanning the vegetation. Grizzly wasn't in sight.

"Cease firing!" Blade ordered as he drew alongside Boone. "Cease firing!"

The forest became abruptly, eerily silent.

"Where's Grizzly?" Blade demanded.

Athena looked around. "I don't know. I saw him just a minute ago."

Blade motioned for Havoc and the Rangers to ford the creek.

"Where is Thunder?" Boone queried, surveying the water. "And what happened to Kraft?"

"I wish I knew," Blade said. He waited for Havoc and the Rangers to reach the east bank. "Okay, people. Listen up. We've got to—"

"There's Grizzly!" Athena exclaimed, pointing.

Blade pivoted in the direction she was indicating.

The mutant was near the large tree 30 feet away. He extended his right forefinger and jabbed it at the ground three times.

"He's found something," Boone remarked.

Blade moved toward Grizzly. "The rest of you stay here. And

stay alert!"

"You don't need to tell me twice," Athena quipped nervously.

Blade hastened over to the mutant. "What's up?"

"I saw you shoot into this tree," Grizzly said. "And I saw something fall. I came over to see if I could find a body."

"Did you?" Blade inquired hopefully.

"Nope," Grizzly replied. "But I did find something else. Something srange."

"Like what?"

"Come see for yourself," Grizzly stated, and moved to the base of the tree. He knelt down. "Take a look at this."

Blade crouched next to the mutant, his eyes narrowing as he beheld a small puddle of greenish fluid on the ground. "What's this?"

"I think it's blood," Grizzly said.

"Green blood?" Blade declared skeptically.

"What else could it be?" Grizzly rejoined. He pointed at another puddle to the north. "I think you hit whatever was in this tree."

"It looks that way," Blade conceded.

"Let me go after it," Grizzly urged.

"No," Blade said, rising.

"No?"

"Come with me," Blade directed. He led the mutant to the bank. "All right. Here's what we're going to do. Grizzly, I want you to find Kraft and Thunder. They fell into the water and were carried downstream around that bend. I couldn't find any sign, but you're a better tracker than I am. You can track by scent." He paused. "We'll follow the trail of blood. It should be easier."

"Grizzly shouldn't go alone," Athena stated. "He can't cover his back and watch the trail at the same time."

"Okay. You go with him," Blade instructed her. "Move it! We'll meet right here in three hours. Understood?"

"Understood," Athena confirmed.

Blade watched the pair jog to the bend and vanish around the curve in the creek. "Follow me," he directed, and returned to the large tree and the puddle of blood.

"That's blood?" Boone queried doubtfully when he saw the liquid.

"It could be," Blade said. "There's some more of it." He

pointed at the second puddle. "I think I hit one of our attackers. We're going to follow this blood, or whatever it is. Boone, stay with me. Havoc and Clayboss to the right, Rivera to the left. Ten-yard spreads. Move!"

Sergeant Havoc and Lieutenant Clayboss headed to the right, Rivera to the left.

"Keep your eyes on them," Blade instructed the frontiersman. He knelt and tentatively placed the tip of his left forefinger in the fluid. The blood, if such it was, was exceptionally thick and sticky.

"What do you figure hit us?" Boone whispered.

"I don't know," Blade said. "But we're going to find out. Right now." He rose and hastened to the north, going from one greenish puddle to the next."

"Whatever the blazes it is," Boone commented, "it's sure losing a lot of blood."

Blade had to agree. He searched the ground for tracks, but the turf was densely packed and covered with grass and weeds. He found sections where the vegetation had been flattened by the passage of a heavy body, but no clear prints. His mind was racing. What in the world had hit them? What type of weapons had their assailants used? And what had happened to Thunder and Kraft? Were they alive . . . or dead? He wondered if he should have sent one of the Rangers with Grizzly and Athena, but it was too late to be second-guessing his own strategy.

The five men cautiously proceeded to the north, covering over half a mile. The thick vegetation hemmed them in, limiting their field of vision. They came to a boulder-strewn hill.

Blade halted, peering upward. The trail of green blood went straight up the middle of the hill, right between two huge boulders. The site reeked of an ambush.

"I don't like this," Boone mentioned.

Blade went to signal for the others to close ranks when he realized the Rangers did not know his new signal for the maneuver. Not unless Havoc had informed them on the flight from Los Angeles. He remembered the Rangers had stopped, along with the rest of the Force when he had given the fist-high sign earlier. So either Havoc had explained the hand signals, or like the professionals they were, the two Rangers had keyed their actions on his. In any event, he didn't have time to waste, so he simply waved the trio in.

They obeyed instantly.

"The blood leads up this hill," Blade whispered. "And it's an ideal spot for a trap. I want a volunteer to go ahead and check."

Sergeant Havoc went to open his mouth, but Lieutenant Clayboss was faster. "On my way," the officer said, and started up the slope.

"Take cover," Blade advised, positioning himself behind a tree, his gaze locked on Clayboss.

The others were secreting themselves behind boulders and trees.

Lieutenant Clayboss climbed slowly up the hill. He held his M-16 in front of him, at the ready. His head swiveled from side to side, and his whole body was tense.

Blade admired the Ranger's courage.

Clayboss reached a point 20 yards up the hill. He was almost to the two huge boulders. He glanced back once and grinned, then stepped higher, his body hunched over to minimize the target he made. He paused and inspected a fresh puddle of green blood, then stopped at the base of the boulders.

The space between the boulders was three feet wide and obscured by shadows.

Blade angled the M60 up the slope, searching for the first trace of trouble.

Lieutenant Clayboss edged into the space between the boulders and disappeared.

Blade waited expectantly.

Seconds elapsed.

The seconds became a minute.

Blade was growing impatient. If Clayboss had been jumped, the Ranger would have had time to get off at least one warning shot. But the hill was shrouded in a deathly quiet.

Another minute dragged by.

Blade was about to break cover and go after Clayboss when someone beat him to the punch.

Sergeant Rivera unexpectedly came around a tree and jogged up the hill toward the boulders.

Blade's lips compressed in annoyance. He knew Clayboss and Rivera were the best of buddies, but their friendship did not justify Rivera's breech of discipline. He went to call out, to call Rivera back, but changed his mind. The shout might alert their enemies.

For a moment it appeared that Rivera's indiscretion had not been a costly mistake.

But the moment passed.

Sergeant Rivera was ten yards up the slope when a streak of red, resembling a miniature arrow in flight, sped from the vicinity of the two huge boulders and lodged in the right side of his neck. Rivera jerked with the impact and dropped to his left knee. He managed to squeeze off a few rounds at the boulder, then toppled backwards, tumbling head over heels for three or four yards and becoming immobile.

Blade wanted to fire but couldn't find a quarry. He detected a blur of red out of the corner of his right eye, and one of the tiny shafts shot past his face. He swung to the right, but all he found were more trees.

This was no good!

There had to be more than one foe, and whoever, or whatever, they were, they evidently knew where the Force fighters were concealed.

"Fall back!" Blade barked, suiting his actions to his words. He sent a half-dozen rounds into the trees to discourage their mysterious adversaries, then retreated for over 40 yards. He finally halted and crouched in the shelter of an enormous log.

Boone and Sergeant Havoc did likewise.

"Why did we run, sir?" Havoc asked in disgust. "We shouldn't have deserted Clayboss and Rivera."

"We had no choice," Blade defended his tactic. "We would have suffered the same fate if we'd stayed there."

"What are they using on us?" Boone queried anxiously. "Guns? I haven't heard a single shot on their side."

"I don't know," Blade responded.

"Are we going back for Clayboss and Rivera?" Sergeant Havoc inquired.

"Yes," Blade assured the noncom. "We're going to circle around that hill and come at these things from the rear. It might give us the element of surprise."

"I don't reckon it will be necessary for us to go to them," Boone commented.

"Why's that?" Blade questioned.

Boone nodded his head to the north. "Because they're coming to us."

Blade glanced to the north.

A half-dozen shadowy figures were skulking toward them through the forest!

CHAPTER SIX

"Do you hear it?" Grizzly asked, his head cocked to one side.

"Hear what?" Athena replied, puzzled.

"The shooting," Grizzly told her. "From the north."

Athena listened, and to her ears wafted the metallic retorts of automatic gunfire. "Blade! It must be Blade!"

"Yep," Grizzly said, then continued to the east.

"Where are you going?" Athena demanded, hesitating for a moment before hurrying to catch up with the mutant.

"I'm following orders," Grizzly stated. "Blade said to find Thunder and Kraft, and that's exactly what I'm going to do."

"But Blade and the others could be in trouble!" Athena declared. "We should help them."

"No way," Grizzly rejoined. "Blade is a big boy. He doesn't need our help. And he's the one who's always drumming into us the importance of following orders. So we're going after Thunder and Kraft."

Athena's anxiety etched lines in her face. "I think we should go to Blade."

"You're here to cover my butt, not to think," Grizzly remarked bluntly, pulling ahead of her.

Athena wavered. The sound of the shooting had ceased, but she was filled with an intuitive feeling of dread for Blade and the rest. Grizzly did have a valid point, though. They were under orders, and Blade was a real stickler for having his orders obeyed. And the lives of Kraft and Thunder were equally as important as the Warrior's. But what if . . .

"Come on!" Grizzly hissed. "We don't have all day!"

Athena reluctantly increased her pace.

"I don't want to lose this trail," Grizzly muttered.

"What trail?" Athena asked. "I don't see anything."

Grizzly snickered. "No offense, but when it comes to tracking, most humans are worthless. They waltz around with their heads up their asses."

Athena smiled sweetly. "No offense, but go shove a grenade up yours."

Grizzly smirked, then knelt to examine a faint impression in the earth.

"What is it?" Athena whispered.

"They're still heading due east," Grizzly informed her. "Towards Grants Pass. There are three of them, moving fast. Two of them are carrying extra weight. Kraft and Thunder."

"How can you tell all of that?" Athena inquired in disbelief.

"Trust me," Grizzly said, standing and resuming their trek. He skirted a tall pine tree. "I found where these three fished the Indian and the shithead out of the water, and I haven't lost them yet." He paused. "And I'm not about to," he added meaningfully.

"You're taking this personally," Athena noted, surveying the landscape.

"Damn straight!" Grizzly snapped. "That ambush was my fault."

"You're nuts," Athena stated.

"I'm serious," Grizzly insisted. "If I'd been on the ball, we would never have been jumped by these turkeys. But I blew it, and Thunder and Kraft have paid the price."

"How did you blow it?"

"I should have picked up an unusual scent, seen a track, something," Grizzly said. "But I didn't."

"Have you picked up a scent yet?" Athena questioned.

"No," Grizzly replied. "But at least I found some tracks. Not complete prints, mind you, but partials. Whatever these things are, they're big, yet light on their feet. I have a feeling I wouldn't have found their trail if they weren't carrying the extra weight."

"What do you think we're up against?" Athena asked nervously.

"That should be obvious," Grizzly answered. "Mutants."

"I know," Athena said. "But what *kind* of mutants?"

"Who knows?" Grizzly rejoined. "The radiation and the chemicals and the wacko scientists made all sorts of freaks. Mutants come in all shapes and sizes. For all we know, we could be after giant ladybugs."

"You don't believe that for a minute," Athena remarked.

"No, I don't. I . . ." Grizzly stopped and held up his right hand. He suddenly crouched.

Athena followed his example, perplexed. She strained her eyes and ears to the maximum, but all she saw was the encircling forest and all she heard was a slight breeze stirring in the trees.

Grizzly raised his head and sniffed the air, then grinned. After a minute he rose and motioned for her to do the same.

"What is it?" Athena asked, her voice barely audible.

"We're close," he told her. "Real close."

"Did you pick up a scent?"

Grizzly nodded. "The wind shifted for a second. I could smell Thunder and Kraft. Kraft's scent came in clear and strong. He always wears that cheap, pukey cologne he bought in LA."

Athena's forehead furrowed. "Kraft bought cologne? Where did he get the money? Cologne is expensive."

"I overheard him bragging to Boone," Grizzly detailed. "Kraft said he bought the cologne on the black market. It's supposed to be a bottle left over from before the war. He claimed it was worth ten times what he paid for it. I saw the bottle. Part of the label is missing. It was called LY-something-or-other."

"Never heard of it," Athena mentioned.

"It reeks," Grizzly said. "But if Kraft wants to walk around smelling like piss, that's his business."

They wound through the undergrowth in silence for over a hundred yards. The trail went into a weed-choked gully.

"Hold up," Grizzly advised.

"What is it?" Athena queried.

"I don't like this. It could be a trap," Grizzly informed her.

"What do we do?"

Grizzly nodded to the left. "We'll work around the gully on this side. If it is a trap, they'll be expecting us to go straight through the middle. So we'll circle all the way around the gully and surprise these bozos."

"Lead the way," Athena said. She diligently stuck with the mutant as he bypassed the gully, and she did her best to make as little noise as possible. Once she inadvertently stepped on a small twig and it snapped.

Grizzly paused and glared at her.

Athena grinned feebly.

Grizzly rolled his eyes and continued.

Athena chided herself over her carelessness. She must do better if she ever hoped to convince Blade to accept her as a member of the Force! And more than anything else, she wanted to join the elite unit. Considering the state of the country, of the entire world, what with all the wild mutants, the mutates, and the evil genetically spawned creatures, not to mention all of the roving bands of plundering humans and other menaces, she knew the Force would see a lot of action. And the Force was her ticket to everything she'd ever wanted. Fame and fortune would be hers! Every story she wrote, every report she filed on their escapades, would constitute another rung on her personal ladder to success. The public would constantly be clamoring for more, and only she, from her insider position, would be able to provide genuine scoops. She would be able to name her own salary!

Grizzly ducked under a low-hanging limb.

As Athena followed suit, she gazed at the mutant's back, at his rippling muscles. Life was strange, sometimes, she philosophized. Who would have ever thought she would strike up a friendship with a mutant? Mutants had always given her the creeps. Initially, she hadn't even liked Grizzly. His arrogance and superior air had rubbed her the wrong way. Besides which, he was an atheist. Although she wasn't nearly as religious as Blade, she did have a generalized faith in a Supreme Spirit, and she had always labeled atheists as egotistical idiots. But here she was, friends with an atheistic mutant!

Grizzly had been right earlier. Their experience in the Kingdom of the Spider had drawn them together. He had saved her life, had charged to her rescue with his claws flashing, and perhaps her overwhelming sensation of gratitude had enabled her to drop her prejudices long enough to see Grizzly for what he really was: a man who happened to be covered with fur and who could revert to a bestial savage at the slightest provocation. But underneath his gruff exterior was a person, someone who wanted companionship yet refused to acknowledge his own need. Grizzly was a hardhead. She would never tell him the truth to his face, but the mutant was exactly like the humans he so despised.

On second thought, maybe that was *why* he despised them.

Athena shook her head to dispel her reverie. Now was hardly the time or place to indulge in idle speculation. Not when there were . . . things . . . lurking in the forest.

Grizzly came to a jumble of fallen trees and effortlessly leaped to the top of one. He turned and offered his left hand to her.

"Take hold," he directed.

Athena reached her right hand up and felt his hairy fingers close on her palm. With startling ease she was hoisted onto the log. Before she quite knew what was happening, Grizzly scooped her into his steely arms and took off across the tumbled trees, vaulting from log to log. The trees had fallen years ago, perhaps downed during a violent storm, and many had lost their limbs. Grizzly's calloused footpads readily secured a purchase on their rough bark. Her breath caught in her throat as he executed a daring 12-foot leap and alighted with a feline grace on the ground.

"There you go," he said, depositing her upon the turf. He noted her expression and chuckled. "What are you trying to do? Use your mouth for a butterfly net?"

Embarrassed, Athena closed her mouth. "Don't ever do that again!" she blurted.

"Why?" Grizzly responded. "I didn't think you got nosebleeds at high altitudes."

"I'm perfectly able to take care of myself," Athena stated. "I didn't need your help."

"I know that," Grizzly said, starting to turn to the east.

"Then why did you carry me over those logs?" Athena demanded.

"Blade gave us three hours to rendezvous with him," Grizzly commented dryly. "Not three years."

"You're a real smartass, you know that?" Athena remarked with a grin.

"I was wondering where my brains were located," Grizzly said.

"It's nice to see you've regained your sense of humor," Athena whispered.

"Wasn't aware I'd lost it," Grizzly quipped.

They were skirting the northern portion of the gully, the verdant incline rearing above them to their right.

Athena raised her left foot to stride over a rock in her path.

Grizzly unexpectedly whirled and sprang, wrapping his right arm around her waist and bearing her to the grass.

"What the . . .!" Athena exclaimed, shocked. Something red streaked past her eyes as she fell.

"Move!" Grizzly growled, hauling her erect. "That way!" he snapped, shoving her in the direction of a stand of trees.

Athena promptly complied, racing for the trees, running a

zigzag pattern.

"Faster, slowpoke!" Grizzly goaded her from behind.

Athena grit her teeth and sprinted as swiftly as her legs would move. She reached the first tree and ducked to the rear as a small crimson shaft struck the trunk with a thump.

Grizzly rounded a tree to her left and pressed his body against the bark.

Athena could feel her legs trembling. She struggled to compose herself, realizing they had walked into another ambush.

"Damn it! They did it to me again!" Grizzly fumed.

"What were they shooting?" Athena queried apprehensively.

Grizzly craned his neck for a quick look-see, then darted from his tree to hers, made a swiping motion with his left arm, and jumped behind the tree again.

"What . . . ?" Athena began.

Grizzly smiled and held his left hand at waist height, palm up. A tiny red arrow rested in his hand.

"What's that?" Athena asked.

Grizzly carefully lifted the shaft higher, inspecting the metal tip and the feathers. "It's a damn dart! The sons of bitches have been using darts on us!"

"Can darts kill?" Athena questioned.

"They can if they're tipped with poison," Grizzly said. "But I don't think these are."

"Why not?"

"Why would these clowns go to so much trouble to lug Kraft and Thunder all over the countryside if they're dead?" Grizzly responded. "Nope. I suspect the bastards are using tranquilizer darts, just like the kind your species uses on animals."

Athena let the dig pass. "But why? Why don't they simply kill us?"

"They must want us alive," Grizzly speculated. "Makes you wonder about the fate they have in store for whoever they capture."

Athena involuntarily shuddered. "I don't want them to capture me!"

"I won't let them," Grizzly promised. He glanced around the tree for a second. "I don't see anything, but I know they're out there."

"I say we get the hell out of here," Athena declared.

"Blade gave us a job to do, remember?"

"We can return and report what we've found out," Athena said. "Then the whole Force can come back and blow these things away."

"We're not returning without Thunder and Kraft," Grizzly vowed.

"How do you propose we save them?" Athena asked. "We can't even get close to these things."

"With you along I can't," Grizzly stated. "I want you to stay put."

"Where are you going?"

"Guess," Grizzly replied, and instantly cut to the right, weaving and dodging, until he was enveloped in the forest.

Silence descended.

Athena gripped her M-16 and gulped. She didn't like this one bit! All the ambition and all the training in the world didn't matter at a time like this! Her life was on the line, and she had to face the simple truth of the matter: She didn't want to die.

Where the hell was that grumpy mutant?

Athena risked poking her head out to scan the gully. Nothing moved. Which didn't mean a thing. She jerked her head back.

Time elapsed.

Five minutes.

Ten.

Athena consulted her watched at 60-second intervals, chafing at the wait.

Come on, Grizzly!

Ten additional minutes went by.

Athena gnawed on her lower lip in frustration. Something was wrong. Terribly, terribly wrong. Grizzly would never leave her alone for so long.

Had the things taken him prisoner?

If they had, what should she do?

Athena pressed her forehead to the bark, suppressing an emotional upthrust of stark fear.

No!

No!

No!

She wasn't about to panic now! When she got down to the nitty-gritty, this was what being on the Force was all about. If she couldn't handle this situation, she might as well chuck her notion of being the ace reporter with the inside scoops on everything the Force did.

So think!

Athena cocked her head, listening, but the forest was quiet. Too quiet. Not even a bird was chirping. She recalled the words of her father, an avid outdoorsman, when he had taken her on her first fishing excursion at the age of ten. "You must always be on the lookout for mutants and worse. Learn to read the animal life. When you can see the small animals going about their business, and you can hear the birds singing, you know you're okay. But if you can't hear the birds, and if there's no sign of the normal wildlife, then watch out!"

Her dear dad had been so wise, so loving!

How she missed him!

There was a loud crack to her rear.

Athena instinctively ducked, the move saving her as another dart smacked into the tree where her head had been a fraction of a second before.

Not today, bozos!

She spun and squeezed the trigger, raking the foliage with a wild burst, chopping leaves from trees and shattering limbs. Without waiting to ascertain the results, she rose and ran in the same direction Grizzly had taken. She calmed her mind, forcing herself to evaluate the odds. There were three of those things out there, according to Grizzly. She knew one of them had circled around her and was now to her rear. The second one was probably on the rim of the gully. Which left one unaccounted for, and he . . . or it . . . was the greatest threat.

Don't blunder into him!

Athena abruptly stopped and crouched alongside a five-foot-tall boulder. Her palms felt sweaty on the M-16. She peered into the undergrowth ahead, hoping she could spot the thing before it spied her.

Show yourself, bastard!

She stiffened as a dark shadow flitted between two trees about 30 yards off. There it was! She waited to see if the thing would show itself, but nothing happened. The one to her rear might be after her, and she couldn't afford to stay in one place for long. She reasoned her best bet would be to keep moving. Her left knee twinged with mild discomfort as she straightened and bore to the left, putting more distance between the gully and herself. Once she escaped, she was going to hurry to the rendezvous point and get Blade and the others. Together they would show. . . .

What was that?

Athena froze at the sight of a furry figure 15 yards to her left, slumped across a low mound. The figure wasn't moving. With mounting trepidation she approached the form. The texture of the light brown fur was unmistakable. She reached the mound and groaned.

Grizzly was lying on his stomach on the mound, his arms draped below his head. Two red darts were imbedded at the nape of his squat neck. Whatever had shot him had probably done so from concealment and from the rear. But why did they use two darts instead of one? Was a stronger dose of their tranquilizer required to down a mutant with Grizzly's iron constitution?

Athena crouched and felt for a pulse on his right wrist.

Forgetting her own predicament.

There was an odd noise behind her, close at hand, resembling a hollow cough.

Athena felt a sharp jabbing sensation on her left shoulder, like being pricked with a pin only worse. She tried to turn, realizing she had foolishly let down her guard.

They'd shot her!

She knew one of the crimson darts was in her shoulder, and dread engulfed her, submerging her in an icy cocoon of fear. Her body abruptly became sluggish, her reflexes languid. The M-16 drooped in her hands, the weapon suddenly weighing a ton.

No!

It wasn't fair!

Athena dropped to her hands and knees, shaking her head to clear her numb mind. She was on the verge of being captured, and she was stunned by the horror of the unknown.

It just wasn't fair!

After spending seven years as a prisoner in the Kingdom of the Spider, to be captured again so soon after achieving her freedom was a travesty of . . . of . . .

CHAPTER SEVEN

Incensed by the ease with which his antagonists were downing his unit, exasperated by his failure to so much as clearly glimpse his foes for a second, and inflamed at being checked at every turn, Blade impulsively rose up from behind the log, leveled the M60, and commenced firing.

The six shadowy figures were over 30 yards away, their features obscured by the vegetation. All of them were toting guns, rifles of an indeterminate type. All of them dived for cover as the Warrior cut loose.

Only four made it.

Two of the creatures were struck by the powerful slugs, their bodies flung backwards. They crashed to the ground, one of them screeching and thrashing convulsively before expiring.

Boone and Sergeant Havoc added their weapons to Blade's, but their enemies were already in hiding.

"Down!" Blade barked, and dropped to his knees.

Boone and Havoc obeyed.

"We're too vulnerable here," Sergeant Havoc commented. "We need a defensible position."

"Or something similar," Blade said. He scurried to a nearby tree and stood, using the tree for cover. A hasty scan confirmed their attackers were nowhere in sight. He motioned for Boone and Havoc to join him.

They promptly complied.

"Stick with me," Blade directed, and ran to the south, retracing their route. He knew the things would be after them soon, maybe in two or three minutes at the most. He needed to find the spot he wanted by then if he was to entertain any hope of turning the tide.

Boone and Sergeant Havoc jogged on the Warrior's heels. They were hard pressed to keep pace with the giant's prodigious strides.

Blade's gray eyes probed the terrain for an ideal site, his mind reflecting on the mission. Pitiful was the only word to describe his performance. He'd led his team into an ambush, then lost two more in another trap. What manner of beings was the Force up against? he wondered. Undoubtedly the things were mutants. Nothing human could have decimated the Force with such uncanny skill. But whatever the things were, they could be killed. And if they could be killed, then the Force stood a chance of winning.

Not much of a chance.

But a chance.

Blade slowed and scrutinized the landscape directly ahead. A boulder approximately six feet in height was situated in a circular clearing ten feet in diameter. High weeds enclosed the clearing. To the right, ten yards from the boulder, was a tree. To the left, 15 yards distant, was another tree.

Perfect.

Blade halted and turned.

Boone and Havoc stopped.

"We're going to use a little reverse strategy," Blade told them. "We've been ambushed twice. Now we'll return the favor."

"What do you want us to do?" Boone inquired.

"I want you to climb that tree," Blade said, pointing at the one on the right. "Havoc, you take that tree on the left. When our ambushers show up, let them have it."

"And where will you be?" Boone asked.

Blade nodded toward the boulder in the clearing. "I'll be the bait to lure them in. If they concentrate on me, they might not notice the two of you in the trees. Wait until you have a clear shot."

"You're taking a big risk, sir," Sergeant Havoc commented.

"There's no other choice," Blade said grimly. "Either we get the upper hand or we're done for."

Sergeant Havoc headed for the tree on the left.

Boone hesitated. "Watch your back."

"I will," Blade promised. "Get going."

Boone dashed to the tree on the right, slung his M-16 over his right shoulder, and began climbing.

Blade hurried to the boulder and moved behind it. If his calculations were correct, there were four foes remaining. Numerically, at least, the odds were almost even. But the creatures evidently knew the country well, and their familiarity gave them a distinct advantage. He peered over the top of the boulder, studying the forest to the north.

The woods conveyed a deceptive impression of tranquility. No evidence of the enemy presented itself.

Blade became impatient for his adversaries to arrive. Over five minutes elapsed.

Four sparrows appeared to the north, flitting from tree to tree.

Five more minutes passed.

A Western Gray Squirrel traipsed along the limbs of a conifer to the northwest.

Blade allowed five additional minutes to elapse before stepping from cover, raising his right arm, and rotating his forefinger in a tight circle.

Boone and Sergeant Havoc descended their trees and hastened to the clearing.

"They should have been here by now, sir," Sergeant Havoc remarked.

"That's what worries me," Blade admitted. "It looks like they didn't come after us."

"Why not?" Boone questioned.

"Let's find out," Blade suggested. He trotted to the north again, feeling perplexed. Why hadn't the things shown up? Had killing two of them dissuaded the rest? He came to the site of the firefight and halted. "This is where I shot those two," he mentioned. "Find their bodies."

The trio searched the vegetation for several minutes.

"The bodies aren't here," Boone mentioned.

"They must have taken them, sir," Sergeant Havoc said.

"Where?" Blade scowled. "I don't like this. We've got to reach that hill as quickly as we can."

They jogged to the north.

"There's the hill," Boone noted as the slope came within view. "But I don't see Rivera."

Blade didn't stop until he was at the exact spot where Rivera had fallen. "They took him! Now they have four of us!"

"Maybe not," Boone said. "Maybe Grizzly and Athena are having better luck than we are. Maybe they found Kraft and Thunder."

"What do we do, sir?" Sergeant Havoc inquired. "Go after them?"

"We try to outguess them," Blade stated. "If I'm right, they're mutants. We know there are mutants in Grants Pass, so we can assume they will be heading there. If we go due east, we should strike their trail. I doubt they can move very fast while carrying the bodies of their dead, plus Rivera and Clayboss."

The three men jogged to the east, ever viligant for their phantom enemies. They covered over a mile, sweat caking their bodies. The temperature rose into the seventies. Without warning, they emerged from a stand of trees and found themselves at the top of a rise. Seventy yards below was a wide field, then more forest.

"Down!" Blade whispered, and flattened. He cautiously inched to the edge of the rise and peered downward.

Four dark green mutants were almost to the forest bordering the field, proceeding to the east. All four were burdened by extra weight; two were bearing a deceased comrade over a broad shoulder, while the other pair were lugging Lieutenant Clayboss and Sergeant Rivera.

"You were right!" Boone said from the Warrior's left.

"Do we take them, sir?" Sergeant Havoc inquired from the right.

"No," Blade said. "We'll follow them."

"If we let them reach Grants Pass, sir," Sergeant Havoc noted, "we might not be able to save Rivera and Clayboss."

"We're not going to let them reach Grants Pass," Blade said. He glanced at the noncom. "And will you stop calling me 'sir'? It's driving me nuts."

"Sorry, sir," Havoc responded.

"Call me Blade," the Warrior directed.

"Yes, sir, Blade. I will," Havoc stated.

Blade looked at the quartet of mutants, striving to distinguish features, but the distance was too great to differentiate precise details.

The four walked into the forest.

Blade checked his watch, calculating. There was still plenty of time before he had to rendezvous with Grizzly and Athena at the creek. Grants Pass was approximately ten miles away. All of which meant he could bide his time before jumping the mutants and rescuing the two Rangers. Consequently, he waited more than three minutes before crawling over the rim of the rise and descending to the field. He searched the woods for mutants before crossing.

The dash to the trees was uneventful.

Blade paused behind a large trunk and scanned the vegetation ahead.

Nothing.

Satisfied the mutants were still hiking eastward, Blade rounded the tree and resumed their pursuit. He toyed with the notion of working his way ahead of the mutants and jumping them when they least expected an attack. Surprise was his edge, and he intended to take full advantage of it.

A half mile went by.

Blade noticed a puddle of greenish fluid on the ground. Was one of the quartet injured, or was the blood from one of the dead mutants? He pressed on until he reached the base of a low hill.

There was no activity on the hill.

Blade walked up the gradual slope, speculating on whether he would find the quartet on the other side.

They were much closer.

Blade, Boone, and Sergeant Havoc were a third of the way up the hill when they heard a scratching noise to their left. As one, they turned.

A trio of green forms had popped up from concealment in a thick stretch of undergrowth, their rifles against their shoulders.

Blade saw a crimson dart flying toward him, and he threw himself to the right in an effort to evade the tiny shaft. He was unsuccessful. The dart caught him high on the left shoulder. He aimed the M60, and as he did so his limbs turned to mush. Whatever the mutants used was fast-acting.

Sergeant Havoc and Boone were down, Havoc to his knees, the frontiersman on his stomach.

Blade grimaced as he forced his right hand to obey his mental command. He squeezed the trigger and the M60 boomed.

One of the mutants was hurled from its feet by the burst.

Two additional darts pierced the giant's skin, one on the neck, the second on his right arm. Blade sagged, swaying from side to side. The M60 fell from his nerveless fingers.

Damn!

He'd blown it!

He'd met his match at last!

Would the mutants slay him while he was unconscious, or did they have a worse fate in store for the Force?

Blade pitched onto his face, engulfed by an equal mixture of guilt and lassitude.

Somewhere, something laughed.

PART THREE
OF REPTILOIDS AND REPTILIAN

CHAPTER EIGHT

"Wake up, you rotten scum! Wake up!"

Blade became dimly conscious of a grating voice bellowing in his left ear. Slowly, so slowly, he regained awareness of his surroundings. He opened his eyes, finding himself on his right side, his wrists bound by heavy rope in front of him. His weapons and his packback were gone.

"So! You're awake at last!" the grating voice barked. "About time, asshole!"

Blade rolled onto his back.

A tall, heavyset man stood three feet away, his face rimmed by a stubbly beard. He sported a thin mustache. His eyes were dark, his cheeks sallow. He wore black pants, a black shirt, and a wide black leather belt. In his right hand was a wooden club two feet in length. "On your feet, bastard!"

Blade's gray eyes narrowed. "Where are my friends?"

The man in black scowled and lashed out with his left foot, his black boot connecting with the giant's ribs.

Blade bent sideways, contorted by the pain.

"I do the talking here!" the tall man declared. "Now on your feet, slime-bucket!"

Blade grit his teeth and straightened. He realized his legs were untied.

"On your feet!" the man shouted. "Or you'll be eating this cudgel!"

"Eat this!" Blade retorted, twisting his body and sweeping his legs up and around. He caught the man in black at the ankles and sent him sprawling onto his back. Blade surged to his knees and pounced.

The tall man was trying to rise when the Warrior slammed into his chest, knocking him to the concrete floor. He attempted to bring his cudgel into play.

Blade, his knees straddling his opponent's chest, blocked the swing of the cudgel with his left elbow. He clasped his hands together, forming a ponderous fist, and savagely smashed the man in black across the chin. Once, twice, three times in all, and the tall man, rocked by Blade's malletlike blows, went limp, his eyelids fluttering.

"Well done, human," someone said to the Warrior's rear.

Blade rose and spun. His eyes widened in amazement and his mouth inadvertently slackened.

"What's the matter, human?" queried the figure near the open wooden door. "Haven't you ever seen a mutant before?"

Blade had, but never one like the dark green figure with a silver pike in its right hand.

The mutant was over six feet in height and conveyed the impression of awesome strength. His skin was a dark green, leathery and muscular. Green pants of the same shade covered its legs. The face and head resembled a reptile's; the eyes were red and emotionless, the nose was elongated, the ears circular. When the creature spoke, pointed teeth were disclosed. Its head was totally hairless.

"What are you?" Blade asked. "Where am I?"

"How original," the mutant quipped.

Blade surveyed the room he was in, noting the four brick walls and the two barred windows. A cot was positioned along one of the walls. "Where am I?" he repeated.

"In the Province," the mutant answered.

"The Province?" Blade repeated, puzzled. "How close am I to Grants Pass?"

The mutant cocked its head and studied the giant for a moment. "You are in Grants Pass," it stated. There was a sibilant accent to its voice. "The Province was once known as Grants Pass. This was decades ago, before the Mutant Era began."

"Where are my friends?" Blade asked.

"They are being held elsewhere," the mutant said. "Reptilian wanted you separated from the rest."

"Who is this Reptilian? And why does he want me separated?"

The mutant grinned, the expression oddly sinister because of its tapered teeth. "All in good time. Reptilian will answer all of your questions during your audience."

"When will I have this audience?" Blade inquired.

"At Reptilian's discretion," the mutant replied. "Perhaps tonight. Perhaps in two days."

"How long was I unconscious?" Blade wanted to know.

"I don't know," the mutant said. "You were unconscious when you were brought to the Imperium."

"What's the Imperium?" Blade queried.

The mutant nodded at the prone man in black. "Revive Prine. He has been assigned as your Indoctrinator." So saying, the creature turned and exited the cell, closing the door behind him. There was a loud rasping noise as a bolt was secured on the outside.

Blade frowned, contemplating his dilemma. He needed answers, lots of answers, and there was only one way to obtain them. He leaned down and retrieved the cudgel from the floor, then shook the man in black.

The man moaned.

Blade shook him again. Harder.

Prine's eyes snapped open. He stared up at the giant, recognition dawning. "You!" he growled, starting to sit up. "I'm going to . . ."

Blade wagged the cudgel in Prine's face. "You're not going to do anything! Make one false move and I'll split your skull!"

Prine looked at the club, then into the giant's eyes. He observed the flinty anger in those gray eyes, and he noted the incredible muscles contouring the giant's shoulders and arms. Somehow, the giant had not seemed so huge while lying on the floor.

"What's it going to be?" Blade demanded. "Do you cooperate or do you die?"

"I don't want to die," Prine said.

"I was told your name is Prine," Blade mentioned.

Prine's forehead creased. "Who told you that?"

"A mutant was just here," Blade disclosed. "He looked like he was part lizard."

Prine blanched. "A mutant? Was it Reptilian?"

"I don't know Reptilian," Blade said.

"Did he see what happened to me?" Prine asked, glancing at the door.

Before Blade could respond, Prine jumped up and moved to the door. He tried to shove it open, to no avail.

"He locked me in here with you!" Prine declared, sounding shocked. "It must have been Reptilian! I'll be slated for premature consumption for sure!"

"Come over here," Blade directed.

Prine gazed at the giant. "Why should I?"

"Because I need you to untie the knots on this rope," Blade said. "I won't harm you."

Prine edged from the door. "What's your name?"

"Blade."

"Listen, Blade," Prine stated nervously. "About the way I treated you earlier . . .."

"What about it?" Blade asked.

"It was nothing personal," Prine said. "I'm expected to treat all new arrivals the same way. If I don't, the Reptiloids will schedule me for premature consumption."

"What is this premature consumption you keep talking about?" Blade inquired. He extended his arms, the cudgel clutched in his hands.

Prine walked over and inspected the rope. "Premature consumption means I'll be eaten ahead of schedule."

Blade did a double take. "Eaten?"

"Sure," Prine confirmed, applying himself to the knots. "The Reptiloids use humans as a food source."

Blade stared at the door. "That's why the mutants capture humans? To eat them?"

Prine nodded while working on the knots.

"I need to know everything there is to learn about this place," Blade stated.

"I'll tell you everything I know," Prine offered. "It's my job as an Indoctrinator to fill all newcomers in."

"That thing with the red eyes said Grants Pass is now called the Province," Blade began.

"Red eyes?" Prine repeated, grinning. "The mutant you saw had red eyes?"

"Yes," Blade verified. "Why? What difference does it make?"

Prine was visibly relieved. "It makes a world of difference. If the mutant you saw had red eyes, then it wasn't Reptilian. His eyes are blue."

"The Reptiloids don't all have the same color eyes?" Blade asked.

"Do humans all have the same color eyes?" Prine countered.

"Tell me about these Reptiloids," Blade said. "Where do they come from? How long have they been in control of Grants Pass?"

Prine tugged on one of the stubborn knots. "The Reptiloids have been here for decades. I don't know exactly how long. Reptilian is their leader. He's the one who renamed Grants Pass as the Province."

"Why the Province?"

Prine shrugged. "Beats me. You can ask him at your audience."

Blade pondered for several seconds. "How many humans are there in the Province?"

"About two thousand," Prine replied.

"And how many of these Reptiloids?"

"About twelve hundred, I think," Prine said.

"If the humans outnumber the Reptiloids, why don't they revolt?" Blade queried.

Prine looked up. "Are you serious? Two thousand unarmed humans wouldn't stand a prayer against the Reptiloids."

"The Reptiloids are well armed?" Blade questioned.

"They have an armory of confiscated weapons," Prine answered. "And some of the sentries carry machine guns. Most of the Reptiloids, though, carry pikes. Those pikes are all they need."

"I don't follow you," Blade confessed.

Prine stared at the giant. "How did you end up here?"

"My unit was captured," Blade disclosed. "We never even saw what hit us." He didn't bother to mention the fact that two of his team, Grizzly and Athena, were still free.

"So how can you wonder why the humans don't revolt?" Prine rejoined. "The Reptiloids don't need to carry guns. One of them is the equal of ten humans. They have super senses. They can hear and smell better than any human. They're twice as strong. And they have their heat detecting ability."

"What's that?" Blade asked.

"I don't know all the details," Prine said. "But I know the Reptiloids can sense body heat from far off."

"Sense body heat? How?"

"I told you I don't know," Prine emphasized. "Ask Reptilian."

"Why haven't you ever asked Reptilian?" Blade queried.

"I've never had an audience with him," Prine said.

"Why am I the lucky one?" Blade questioned.

Prine paused in his effort to undo the knots. "You must be special."

"In what way?"

"Reptilian only sees the special humans," Prine stated. "The ones with the qualities he wants."

"What qualities?"

"Ask him," Prine said. He rose and nodded toward Blade's wrists. "There you go."

Blade glanced down to find the knots untied. He deftly swirled his arms and the rope fell to the floor.

"Now you owe me one," Prine declared.

"I'd say we're about even," Blade said, disagreeing.

"I have to rough the arrivals up," Prine asserted. "If I don't, I'm in deep shit."

"Are there other Indoctrinators?" Blade asked.

Prine nodded.

"For someone who's supposed to fill me in," Blade remarked, "you haven't told me a lot."

Prine shrugged. "I've done the best I could. The Reptiloids don't blab all their secrets to humans, you know."

"How long have you been here?" Blade inquired.

"About eleven years," Prine revealed.

"You've lasted that long without being eaten?" Blade commented.

"If you serve the Reptiloids without giving them any hassles," Prine stated, "you last longer. The average is about five years."

"So you're a good little slave," Blade said, his tone registering his disgust.

Prine was offended. "What do you expect me to do? Fight back? What chance would I have? I'd be eaten tomorrow. And I sure as hell wouldn't be stupid enough to try and escape. I wouldn't last two hours out there with a Hunter Squad on my trail."

"What's a Hunter's Squad?"

"That's probably what bagged you and your friends," Prine mentioned. "The Hunter Squads go out after humans. They use tranquilizer darts."

Blade nodded. "A Hunter Squad caught us, all right. But we got in a few licks of our own."

Prine placed his hands on his hips. "How do you mean?" he inquired idly.

"I killed two or three of them," Blade divulged.

Prine's mouth fell open. "You killed Reptiloids?"

"Yes," Blade said.

Prine shook his head. "I wouldn't want to be in your shoes."

"Why not?"

"Killing a Reptiloid is a cardinal offense," Prine stated. "It's certain death."

"Then I have nothing to lose," Blade commented. He walked over to the wooden door and examined the jamb.

"What are you talking about?"

"If killing a Reptiloid is certain death," Blade said, "then I'm as good as dead. Unless I escape."

Prine snickered. "No one has ever escaped from the Provincel"

"One man has," Blade corrected him. "He escaped and reached California. That's why I'm here."

"California?" Prine said excitedly. "I was on my way to California from eastern Washington when the Reptiloids caught me."

"I was sent here to free the humans," Blade detailed. "And to terminate Reptilian."

"You're doing a great job so far," Prine cracked.

"I'm just getting started," Blade assured him. "I take it you know where I'm being held?"

"Sure," Prine responded. "You're on the top floor of the Imperium, at ground level."

Blade gazed at the barred window to his right. "How can the top floor be on ground level?"

"Because most of the Imperium is underground," Prine explained. "The Reptiloids prefer to live underground. They don't much like the bright sunlight. Oh, they'll send out Hunter Squads for a day or two at a time. And they guard us during the day when we're tilling the fields and working on their projects. But, generally speaking, they like underground better."

Blade looked at the floor. "So the Imperium is under our feet?"

"Yep," Prine confirmed. "It goes about ten stories underground. That's not counting the Arena."

"What's that?"

"Believe me," Prine said. "You don't want to know."

"Where are my friends being held?" Blade asked.

"Probably on this level," Prine replied. "This is where they hold all the new arrivals."

"Good!" Blade smiled. "Get set."

"Set for what?"

Blade stared at the door. A barred window, six inches square, was situated near the top. He peered out the window at a gloomy corridor, insuring none of the Reptiloids were in sight.

"Set for what?" Prine reiterated.

Blade turned and stepped to the far side of the cell. He faced the door and squared his shoulders.

"Set for what?" Prine demanded in annoyance.

Blade grinned. "For this." He charged toward the door at top speed, his left shoulder lowered to absorb the brunt of the collision. His huge body smashed into the center of the door with a tremendous crash, jarring the door to its frame. The door buckled outward and cracked down the middle but remained in place. His shoulder throbbing, Blade drew his right leg up and delivered a shattering kick.

The door splintered and toppled into the corridor.

Prine was gaping at the doorway. "How'd you do that?" he blurted in astonishment.

"Let's go!" Blade ordered.

"Go? Where?"

"You're going to find my friends," Blade directed. "Now!"

"The Reptiloids will kill me!" Prine protested.

Blade lowered his voice and hefted the cudgel. "And what do you think will happen to you if you don't?"

Prine balked, obviously terrified at the prospect of resisting the Reptiloids.

"Move it!" Blade snarled.

Frowning, reluctant to comply, Prine shuffled forward.

Blade grabbed the man in black by the left elbow and pushed him into the corridor. "Move it! Or else!"

Prine nervously glanced in both directions. "They must be in one of the larger holding cells." He took off to the right.

Blade stayed close to the Indoctrinator. He didn't trust the man for a second. Prine would turn him in or betray him at the first opportunity, and Blade wasn't about to give the man the chance.

The floor of the corridor was composed of brown tile and the walls were plaster. Illumination was supplied by regularly spaced lanterns affixed to metal holders on the walls. There were no windows, but other cell doors were spaced at 20-yard intervals.

"It shouldn't be far," Prine said.

Blade looked to the rear. He was surprised none of the mutants had shown up yet. Surely they would have heard the racket when he busted out of his cell? Why hadn't they sent someone to investigate?

"This way," Prine stated, taking a turn to the left.

Blade cautiously followed, alert for the first hint of treachery. He disliked relying on the Indoctrinator, but what choice did he have? Searching the entire floor by himself was out of the question. The mutants would find him before he was done.

"It should be two doors down," Prine commented.

Off in the distance was a loud shout.

Prine reached a closed door. "Here it is!" he declared, grabbing the doorknob and yanking the door open. "Your friends are in here!"

Eager to find his companions and concerned for their welfare, Blade hastened past Prine and entered the cell without bothering to verify the cell was occupied.

It wasn't.

Blade realized his mistake as he heard the door slam shut behind him. He spun and rammed his right shoulder against the inner wooden panel, but the door held.

Prine's triumphant face filled the small window in the door. "You should be saving your strength! You're going to need it when you see Reptilian."

Blade was about to try and break down the door when three Reptiloids materialized behind the man in black.

Prine threw back his head and laughed.

CHAPTER NINE

Why were his wrists hurting so much?

Sergeant Havoc opened his eyes, and for a moment he was under the impression he was dreaming. He was in a square cell, his wrists in shackles, chained to a brick wall with his boots dangling six inches above the floor. No wonder his wrists hurt!

"Welcome to the world of the living," commented someone to his left.

Sergant Havoc twisted his neck. At the sight of Boone, who was also shackled to the wall, his memories returned in a rush. He recalled the drop in the Siskiyou National Forest and the subsequent fight with the unseen assailants.

"How are you feeling?" the frontiersman asked.

"I feel okay," Havoc answered.

"I've been awake for a few minutes," Boone said. "Blade isn't here, but we do have company."

Sregeant Havoc gazed to the right.

Other Force members were likewise chained to the wall. Thunder was to the noncom's right, then Kraft, then Sergeant Rivera.

"Where are the others?" Havoc inquired.

"We don't know," Boone said.

"They could be dead," Kraft interjected.

"We must find them," Havoc stated.

"Yeah, sure! How are we supposed to do that, Joe Army?" Kraft snapped. "In case you hadn't noticed, dude, we're not going anywhere! All of our guns are gone and they took our backpacks! And how are we going to get out of these chains? Gnaw through them with our teeth?"

"Where there's a will, there's a way," Sergeant Havoc stated.

Kraft laughed. "What a crock!"

"Pay him no heed," Thunder said, addressing the noncom. "He speaks with the voice of youth and immaturity."

Kraft glared at the Flathead Indian. "Who the hell are you

calling immature, turkey?"

Thunder smirked. "If the moccasin fits . . ."

Sergeant Rivera finally entered the conversation. "Hey! Do you guys argue like this all the time?"

"Not all the time," Boone answered. "Just when we're awake."

Rivera glanced at Havoc. "I thought you were in an elite unit. If you ask me, the Force isn't worth spit."

Kraft bristled. "Yeah? Who asked you, greaser?"

Sergeant Rivera's face turned a faint shade of red. He glowered at the blond youth in the black leather attire. "Greaser? Nobody calls me that! You just made the biggest mistake of your life! When I get down from here, I'm going to stomp your sissy white ass."

"You and what army?" Kraft retorted.

A new voice intruded on their dispute, a low, sibilant, mocking voice. "Such togetherness! The human species is one big, happy family, isn't it?"

As one, their eyes focused on the opposite side of the large room. As one, they gaped at the creature framed in the doorway, at his dark green hide, his red eyes, and his grotesque lizardlike features.

The mutant motioned with the gleaming pike he held in his right fist. "Are we having fun?" he taunted them.

"Who are you?" Sergeant Havoc demanded. "Why are you holding us like this?"

"Please," the lizard-man said condescendingly. "Don't insult my intelligence. You know why we are holding you. Because you, and your associates, were engaged in a hostile act of aggression against the Province."

Havoc went to speak, but the mutant cut him off.

"Don't deny it!" the creature stated. "Why else would an armed group be heading toward our city? We were fortunate one of our Hunter Squads intercepted you."

"Who are you?" Sergeant Havoc asked.

"I am called Gat," the mutant replied. "I am the Prefect here, second in command to Reptilian and his principal adviser. I wanted to observe you for myself. This is a very exceptional case."

Havoc didn't understand half of what the mutant was saying, but he needed information and wanted the creature to keep talking. Tact and diplomacy were called for. "There were others with us. Do you happen to know what happened to them?"

"I saw one of your colleagues a while ago," Gat revealed. "The big one. Your leader, I believe."

"Blade?" Kraft interjected. "Where is he?"

"Elsewhere," Gat replied. He studied the five humans for a minute. "You would make interesting contestants. I will recommend such a disposition to Reptilian."

"Will you let us down from here?" Havoc queried.

"In due time," Gat answered. He turned to leave.

Two more mutants appeared in the hallway. They exchanged whispers with Gat, who then reentered the cell.

"We need a volunteer," Gat stated, grinning.

"For what?" Havoc inquired.

"It seems the first one we took was not sufficient for our needs," Gat declared. "Another one of you is required."

"You took one of us?" Havoc asked, perturbed.

"Yes," Gat said. He indicated an empty set of shackles to the right of Sergeant Rivera with a jab of his pike. "A soldier. He said his name was Clayboss."

Rivera was all attention. "Lieutenant Clayboss? You know where he is?"

"Indeed I do," Gat confirmed, absently rubbing his abdomen with his left hand.

"And you need a volunteer to join Clayboss?" Sergeant Rivera questioned hopefully.

"Yes," Gat said.

"I'll go," Rivera offered.

Gat smiled. "Are you certain you want to go?"

"Sí," Rivera assured the mutant. "Yes. I want to join Clayboss."

Gat smirked. "Just so you're certain." He nodded at the pair behind him and they walked toward the Ranger.

Havoc looked at his friend. "I don't think this is such a good idea."

"I must find Clayboss," Rivera said. "Us Rangers stick together. You know that."

Sergeant Havoc watched the two lizard-men release Rivera. One of the mutants retrieved a small stool from a corner of the cell. He used the stool to stand on while unlocking the Ranger's shackles.

Rivera dropped to his feet, wobbled for a moment, then straightened.

"You will follow me," Gat directed, exiting the room.

Rivera glanced up at Havoc as he walked across the cell. He grinned and winked confidently.

Sergeant Havoc felt his stomach muscles inadvertently constrict as the cell door banged shut.

"I wouldn't trust those things as far as I can throw a horse," Boone commented.

"What a dork!" Kraft stated sarcastically. "I would never have done that."

Sergeant Havoc's chains rattled as he faced the Clansman. "No, *you* wouldn't!" he said bitterly. "And do you know why? Because you don't know the meaning of the word friendship! You don't know what it means to commit yourself to others. The only duty you have is to yourself. It's you first, and everyone else second. You're selfish and you're stupid. You don't deserve to be on the Force."

"Do you think I want to be in this bullshit outfit?" Kraft countered. "I didn't come all the way to California from Minnesota to get snuffed by a bunch of lizards! I knew there'd be fighting, but I like to rumble. I didn't expect all this military garbage. I could be lying on a beach right now, a fox on each arm, instead of hanging here and waiting to get my balls racked."

"This constant bickering must stop," Thunder remarked, gazing from the noncom to the Clansman. "We are a team, remember? We must put our personal animosities aside." He locked eyes with Kraft. "None of us are happy about being here. All of us miss our homes. I know I miss the forests of western Montana. Life there is relatively peaceful. We have mutant problems, but who doesn't?" He paused, a faraway look to his dark eyes. "I miss the smell of the pine trees in the early morning and the cool breeze off of Flathead Lake. I miss hunting and trapping and the aroma of a blacktail buck roasting over an open fire. I miss my family, my father and mother, two sisters and three brothers, and the happy times we shared. I am not comfortable living in the white man's world." He sighed. "No, Kraft. You are not the only one who is unhappy here."

"I miss Dakota," Boone mentioned wistfully. "I miss the feeling you get when you're on your favorite mount, galloping over the plains with the wind in your hair. I miss sitting around a campfire at night, slinging the bull with my friends. I miss those wild Dakota women, who can teach a man things about himself he never suspected existed. I miss the freedom I had there. In California I feel so hemmed in all the time." He glanced at the noncom. "What about you?"

"I was born and raised in California," Sergeant Havoc said. "My grandfather and my father were both career military men. I simply followed in their footsteps. The service is my life. I don't care which branch or unit I'm in. Being assigned to the Force, though, has been a bit of a letdown."

"Why's that, dude?" Kraft queried scornfully. "Aren't we good enough for you?"

Sergeant Havoc stared at the Clansman. "One of you leaves a lot to be desired. Guess who?"

"Up yours!" Kraft snapped.

"Here we go again," Boone muttered.

"I tried," Thunder stated.

They lapsed into an uncomfortable silence, each of them immersed in his own troubled thoughts. Periodically they strained at their shackles, a futile gesture because the chains were clearly unbreakable. They lost all track of the passage of time.

"I'm hungry," Kraft announced, breaking the silence. "When are those freaks going to feed us?"

"Leave it to you to think of eating at a time like this," Sergeant Havoc remarked.

"Don't start!" Boone interrupted them. "We should be working on a way to break out of here instead of squabbling."

The cell door abruptly flew open and in walked the mutant named Gat. He was attended by the same pair of mutants as before, both of whom were carrying trays laden with food.

Gat gazed at the prisoners, grinning. "You must be famished. I have brought some nourishment."

"All right!" Kraft said, elated.

"I'm not hungry," Havoc informed the mutant.

"Neither am I," Thunder said.

"I'll pass," Boone added.

"What a pity," Gat said. "I've brought meals for all of you. You really should keep up your strength for the Arena." He slowly moved closer to the captives. "Won't you reconsider?"

Sergeant Havoc, Boone, and Thunder did not respond.

"I'll eat!" Kraft declared. "Bring on the food!"

Gat stared at the Clansman. "You might not like the meal we have prepared."

"I don't care what it is," Kraft said. "I'm starving!"

"Very well," Gat stated, smirking. "Let him down," he said to the other two mutants.

The pair of attendants moved to a cot positioned along the right-hand wall and deposited their trays. They used the stool to release the Clansman.

Kraft fell the six inches to the floor, his knees buckling under him. He steadied himself before he could fall and stood. "Damn! My shoulders hurt!" he complained.

Gat waved his pike toward the cot. "Some sustenance will help you forget your discomfort."

Kraft grinned as he advanced to the cot, alternately rubbing his sore wrists. "Far out! What a feed!"

"Help yourself," Gat said. "You will find a pitcher of water. There are also potatoes, bread, and a rare treat. I had a can of peaches opened especially for this occasion."

Kraft sat down on the cot. He licked his lips as he regarded the feast. "This is great! Where did you get all this stuff?"

"The humans in the Province grow most of their own food," Gat detailed. "We also have a store of canned goods left over from before the war. The canned goods are quite remarkable. We discovered they will keep for ages if you store them in a cool area. We store ours in a subterranean level of the Imperium."

Kraft picked up a small circular roll containing a patty of cooked ground meat. "This smells funny. What is it?"

Gat smiled. "That is one of our specialties. It's called a burger."

Kraft raised the roll to his nose and sniffed. "What kind of meat is this? It doesn't small like beef or venison."

"It is a mixture of meats," Gat said. "We eat them all the time. Try it. You'll like it."

Kraft shrugged and bit into the burger. He chewed tentatively for a minute, then smiled and swallowed. "This ain't half bad! I could grow to like this."

Gat nodded, his lips upcurled. "Eat hearty. We want you strong and fit for the Arena."

"What is this Arena?" Sergeant Havoc inquired.

"You will find out soon enough," Gat said.

"Don't answer me then," Sergeant Havoc stated. "But don't expect us to answer any of your questions."

Gat looked at the trooper. "You will not be questioned. We already have all the information we require."

"Sure you do," Sergeant Havoc said.

Kraft finished cramming the first burger into his mouth and selected a second.

"We know all we need to know," Gat maintained. "We know your unit is designated as the Force. We know you were sent to free the humans held in the Province and to assassinate Reptilian. You will fail on both counts."

Havoc, Boone, and Thunder exchanged puzzled glances.

"How do we know so much about you?" Gat interpreted their expressions. "Simple. Lieutenant Clayboss and Sergeant Rivera gladly supplied the information."

"I don't believe it," Sergeant Havoc said. "Clayboss and Rivera are Rangers. You could never make them talk."

Gat smiled maliciously. "There are ways, Sergeant Havoc."

"You know my name?" Havoc asked, consternation creasing his brow.

"I know all of your names," Gat declared. "The Indian is named Thunder, the other one Boone." He swiveled and faced the Clansman. "And this simpleton stuffing his face is called Kraft."

Kraft had finished polishing off the second burger. "Get bent, freak!" He reached for a third burger.

Sergeant Havoc glanced from Kraft to the mutant. Something was wrong here. Terribly wrong. He could feel it, but he couldn't put his finger on it. Gat was too smug, as if he was privy to a fact the rest of them didn't know. "Where are Clayboss and Rivera now?"

Gat looked at Havoc. "We finished our interrogation, so I brought them back to the cell."

"Did you leave them in the hallway?" Boone queried.

"No," Gat said, his eyes twinkling. "I brought them back to this cell."

"What kind of game are you playing?" Havoc demanded. "Clayboss and Rivera aren't here."

"Ahhh. But they are," Gat asserted. He took several strides toward the cot. "Are you eating your fill?"

Kraft had taken a few bites from the third burger. "Yeah. These burgers are great."

Gat grinned. So did the other two mutants.

"May the Great Spirit preserve us!" Thunder unexpectedly stated.

Sergeant Havoc looked at the Flathead. "What's wrong?"

Gat snickered. "Your astute Indian friend has perceived the truth. My compliments, Thunder."

Kraft was listening to their discussion in evident confusion. "The truth about what?" he asked, his mouth full of burger.

Gat stared at the Clansman. "It seems I have been slightly remiss. Since you like those burgers so much, perhaps you would appreciate learning the ingredients."

"Who cares?" Kraft rejoined. "Just so they taste good."

"You might care," Gat said. "I was not lying when I told you Lieutenant Clayboss and Sergeant Rivera were in this cell. You see, they're on those trays. At least, parts of them are."

Kraft was about to take another bite from the burger. He paused, the roll and the patty inches from his mouth. "What?"

"When I said the burgers are a mixture of meats, I was also telling the truth," Gat remarked with scarcely suppressed mirth. "The burgers are an equal mixture of Lieutenant Clayboss and Sergeant Rivera."

Kraft let go of the burger like it was a scorching hot coal.

"There wasn't much of Clayboss left after the jail guards had their meals," Gat said. "But there was enough to mix with Rivera's meat to make a batch of delicious burgers."

Kraft's eyes widened in rapidly dawning horror.

"Dear God!" Boone exclaimed in revulsion.

Kraft reached his right hand up and touched his lips. "You're putting me on!" he declared weakly.

"Would I lie to you?" Gat responded. "I wouldn't want to be accused of being an impolite host." He started laughing.

The pair of attendants joined in.

"No!" Kraft cried. "Oh, no!" He rose from the cot and backed away, gawking at the trays.

"Oh, yes," Gat said, beaming.

Kraft's features were transformed by his overwhelming

loathing. He paled, his stomach churning.

"I love it!" Gat stated, and cackled. "They always act the same way!"

Kraft suddenly sank to his knees and doubled over, gagging.

Gat turned toward the doorway. "This is the disgusting part. I can't stand the sight of human vomit."

The three mutants walked to the door. One of the attendants handed a key to Gat.

"Here is the key to your shackles," the Prefect said. He tossed the key onto the cell floor. "When Kraft is finished, he can release all of you. We want you limber for the Arena." He laughed as he exited.

The cell door closed with a bang.

"Dear God!" Boone declared again, his eyes on the Clansman.

Kraft was gasping, his hands pressed to his abdomen, spittle dribbling from his mouth. "No!" he wailed. "No!"

Sergeant Havoc closed his eyes and swallowed. Hard.

Thunder averted his gaze from the Clansman.

For the longest while the only sound in the cell was that of a man in torment, a man whose anguish was unbearable, a man who was puking his guts out.

For the longest while.

CHAPTER TEN

He came awake instantly, his senses fully alert, and automatically leaped to his feet prepared to do battle.

"Calm down, Grizzly. I'm the only one here."

Grizzly slowly relaxed as he surveyed the cell they were in; the cement floor, the brick walls, and the cot along the left-hand side. A solitary barred window was to his right.

Athena was seated on the cot. "You were out a lot longer than I was," she commented, rising.

"Are you all right?" Grizzly asked her.

"Fine," Athena said. "Just worried."

Grizzly moved to the door and peered through the small barred window at the corridor beyond. "I don't see anyone."

"No one has been here since I woke up," Athena mentioned.

"We've got to break out of here," Grizzly said.

"That door looks pretty sturdy," Athena commented.

"We'll see," Grizzly said. He tensed, his keen ears detecting the pad of feet in the corridor. "We've got company." He gazed through the window and spied three figures approaching.

"Who is it?" Athena queried anxiously.

Grizzly retreated from the door, giving himself room to maneuver. He stood in the center of the cell with Athena to his left.

The cell door slowly opened and a mutant entered. He smiled at them, his red eyes flicking from one to the other. "Greetings. I am Gat. I'm pleased to see both of you have recovered from the tranquilizer." Two similar mutants were visible over his shoulders.

Athena calmly scrutinized the lizard-men. "Are you the one who captured us, ugly?"

"No. A Hunter Squad brought you in," Gat said. "All of you."

"All of us?" Athena repeated quizzically.

"Yes. Everyone on the Force has been taken prisoner," Gat revealed. He rested the shaft of his pike on the floor.

Athena shook her head. "I don't believe you."

"How else would I know all about you?" Gat queried. He stared at Grizzly. "We were surprised to find a fellow mutant among our enemies. We accorded you the privilege of having your female in your cell."

"*His* female?" Athena snapped, about to berate the lizard-man. Grizzly held up his right hand, hushing her. "I am Grizzly."

"I know," Gat said. "I know all of your names."

"How do you know so much about us?" Grizzly inquired.

"We interrogated two of the human sent to assassinate our leader," Gat explained. "Humans, as you probably know, are pathetically weak. They spilled the beans, as their kind would say."

"Why are you treating me so courteously?" Grizzly questioned suspiciously. "I too was sent to assassinate your leader."

Gat studied Grizzly for a moment. "You are a mutant, like us. You are of the superior species. We prefer to extend to you the benefit of the doubt. Perhaps your stay among the humans has warped your thinking. Perhaps they have succeeded in turning you against your own kind. We shall see."

"Are the other Force members still alive?" Grizzly asked.

"Some of them," Gat answered.

"*Some* of them?" Athena interjected apprehensively. "Which ones?"

Gat ignored her question. "You really must teach your female her proper place," he said to Grizzly. "Her arrogance is annoying. In the New Order such behavior will not be tolerated."

"The New Order?" Grizzly repeated quizzically.

"Reptilian will explain everything to you," Gat said. "You will have the option of joining our great cause or not."

"Reptilian is your leader?" Grizzly asked.

Gat nodded. "You will be granted an audience in a day or so. Until then, we are compelled to keep you in this cell. I apologize, but you must understand our position. We must test your loyalty to the mutant cause before we can grant your freedom."

"I understand," Grizzly said.

"Excellent," Gat commented. He cast a disdainful glance at Athena, then turned to leave. "Oh. Before I forget." He looked at Grizzly. "I will be posting a guard outside your door. If you need anything, let him know. And I will have a tray of food sent up."

"Thanks," Grizzly said politely.

Gat departed with his escort.

Athena waited until the cell door was closed before she vented her annoyance. "What the hell was that all about?"

"I don't know what you're talking about," Grizzly replied innocently.

"Like hell you don't!" Athena said. "Why were you so nice to that bastard? And why did you let him think I'm your woman?"

Grizzly walked to the window and stared out at an expanse of green lawn. "I had my reasons."

"I'd like to hear them," Athena stated.

Grizzly faced her. "We are in serious trouble here. All of us have been captured and some of us have been killed. . . ."

"If lizard-lips was telling the truth," Athena interrupted.

"I believe he was," Grizzly said. "I also suspect he would kill you without hesitation if he knew you're not my woman."

"So that's why you went along with him?" Athena said.

"Partly," Grizzly verified. "I didn't want to do anything to anger him or arouse his suspicion. We have to find the others, and we may get the chance if Gat grants me the run of this place."

"We're taking a big risk," Athena remarked. "The others could all be dead by then."

"What else would you have me do?" Grizzly queried. "If I made my play now, we would probably be caught again. And then the others would be worse off than before. This way, if I suck up to these scumbags, if they allow us to go free, we can find the others and help them escape."

"I hope you're right," Athena said doubtfully.

"At least we have an ace in the hole," Grizzly stated.

"We do?"

Grizzly held up his hands and straightened his fingers. Instantly his retractable claws popped out and locked in place, extending five inches above the tips of his nails. "These are our ace in the hole," he said. "Gat and his pals don't know about my claws. When the time comes, I'll be sure they get acquainted." He grinned wickedly, relaxing his fingers, and the claws slid from view.

Athena stared at him with an odd expression on her face.

"What is it?" Grizzly inquired.

"I just had a thought," Athena mentioned. "I think you're lying to me."

"You're my friend," Grizzly declared. "I would never lie to you."

"But you might fib to spare my feelings," Athena said. "And you're fibbing now. The real reason you're sucking up to these cruds is because of me, isn't it?" \

"I don't know what you're talking about," Grizzly remarked.

"Bet me!" Athena countered. "You could break out of here any time you wanted. These lizard-men wouldn't be able to stand up to your claws. The real reason you're staying is because of me. I would be a hindrance if you tried to escape with me in tow. So you're sticking it out until you can get both of us out of here. Am I right?"

"That's the trouble with writers," Grizzly quipped. "You all have an overactive imagination."

"Yes or no?" Athena persisted. "Are you holding back because of me?"

"No," Grizzly said.

"I don't believe you," Athena told him.

Grizzly sighed. "Not to change the subject, but now I know why I couldn't pick up their scent earlier."

"Why's that?"

"They don't have any scent," Grizzly said. "Their body odor is virtually nil. I've encountered the same thing in snakes and lizards. It makes me feel a little better about myself. For a while there, I thought I was losing my touch."

The cell door swung wide, admitting two lizard-men. One bore a tray of food, the other carried a pike. The mutant with the tray crossed to the cot and placed it down. "Here. With Gat's regards."

"Thank him for me," Grizzly said.

The pair left.

Athena walked to the cot and examined the tray. "This doesn't look half bad. We've got some veggies and hamburgers."

"Hamburgers?" Grizzly repeated, coming forward.

"Yeah. That's right. You're not from California. You've probably never enjoyed a hamburger before," Athena said. She grabbed one of the burgers and handed it to Grizzly. "Here. Chow down on this."

Grizzly took the burger and lifted the roll to his nose.

Athena took one of the burgers and licked her lips as she raised it to her waiting mouth. "I'm so hungry I could eat a horse." She opened her mouth to take a bite.

"No!" Grizzly cried, lashing out with his left arm and knocking the burger from her fingers.

Athena gaped at him in amazement. "What the hell did you do that for?"

Grizzly's eyes narrowed as he examined his burger. "I didn't think you're a cannibal."

"What?"

Grizzly wagged his burger. "The meat here is human."

Athena's mouth went slack. "Human? Are you sure?"

Grizzly tapped his nostrils. "The nose knows."

Athena looked down at the tray, her shock showing. "They fed us burgers of humans?" she said, aghast.

Grizzly deposited his burger on the tray. "Afraid so. Maybe it's Gat's idea of a little joke."

Athena blinked rapidly several times. "I can't believe it! why?"

"The answer should be obvious," Grizzly responded.

Athena gazed at him, her eyes wide. "They eat . . . human flesh."

"Looks that way," Grizzly stated. He was startled when she unexpectedly stepped up to him and threw her arms around his neck.

"Dear Lord!" Athena exclaimed. "I almost ate one."

Grizzly could feel her trembling as she hugged him. "But you didn't."

Athena abruptly released him and moved back. "What if . . . it's one of the Force?"

"We have no way of knowing that," Grizzly said, trying to ease her mental anguish.

"Can't you tell? Your nose, I mean," Athena mentioned.

"Nope," Grizzly replied. "Cooked meat doesn't have the same scent as before it's cooked."

Athena gazed at the window. "We've got to get out of here!"

"We will," he assured her.

"What if they do that to me?" Athena queried, pointing at the tray.

"I won't let them," Grizzly promised.

Athena shuddered. "God! I wish I'd never come along on this

mission."

"We'll get out of here," Grizzly reiterated. "I'll stake my life on it."

"You may have to," Athena said somberly. "We both may have to."

Grizzly shrugged. "What's life without a little challenge now and then?"

CHAPTER ELEVEN

Blade paced his cell like a caged cougar. The longer he paced, the madder he became. He was furious at himself for his failure, and he craved vengeance on the creatures responsible for capturing most of the Force. By his estimation, he'd spent over 24 hours in the cell. Twice the Reptiloids had offered him a tray of food; each time he had declined. Four mutant guards had been posted outside of his door. Their first act had been to take his cudgel. Prine had disappeared after tricking him into entering the cell.

Prine would get his! Blade pledged.

What was that?

There was the scratching of a bolt being thrown, and seconds later the door opened. In strolled the mutant Blade had seen once before, the Reptiloid with the red eyes, his pike in hand.

"Hello, Blade," the mutant greeted him.

"Did Prine tell you my name?" Blade demanded.

"No," the mutant replied. "Lieutenant Clayboss did. My name, by the way, is Gat."

"Where is Clayboss?" Blade asked. "And the rest of my unit?"

"They are nearby," Gat said. "And they have not been harmed. You will be able to see them, in time."

"How much time? When do I get to see Reptilian?" Blade queried angrily.

"Soon," Gat replied. "Very soon."

"How do I know my people are all right?" Blade inquired. "How do I know I can trust you?"

"You must simply take my word for it," Gat assured the giant.

Blade scowled.

"The guards tell me you have not eaten," Gat observed. "Why not?"

"I haven't been hungry," Blade said.

"You must be famished," Gat disagreed. "We have not poisoned your food, if that's what you're worried about. And starving yourself to death would be a terrible waste."

"I'll eat when I'm good and ready," Blade snapped.

Gat, strangely, smiled. "You have fire in your veins. Such a commendable quality!"

Blade gazed past Gat at the corridor. The four guards were lounging near the doorway, apparently bored with their task. None of them, evidently, entertained the idea he might attempt to escape. Perhaps escapes were rare; all four had propped their pikes against the hall wall.

Their mistake.

"Well, when you are hungry, let me know," Gat was saying. He started toward the door.

"Say, Gat," Blade said.

Gat stopped and partially turned, his eyes narrowing slightly. "Yes?"

"Maybe I could use some food," Blade told him.

Gat grinned. "Fine. I'll have some burgers sent up." He strolled to the door.

Blade tensed, girding his massive muscles. He waited until Gat was between the jambs, until the mutant was in midstride in the doorway, blocking the view of the guards in the corridor. With their field of vision obstructed, he would be on them before they knew it.

He charged.

Blade plowed into Gat, driving his right shoulder into the small of the mutant's back and sending Gat flying straight into the guards.

Two of the guards were knocked to the floor with Gat sprawled on top of them.

The other pair closed on the giant, neglecting to use their pikes.

Blade knew the lizard-men possessed immense strength, but so did he. And he enjoyed the distinct advantage of superior size; each of the lizard-men stood about six feet in height, while he was a giant among men at seven feet. In addition, his long arms gave him the greater reach. Now, as they came at him from both sides, he employed his advantages to the fullest.

One of the lizard-men hissed as it lunged, the one on the right.

Blade whipped his torso in a tight arc, ramming his right elbow into the face of the mutant on the right. There was an audible crunch and the Reptiloid was catapulted backwards to crash onto its back, green blood spewing from its crushed nose.

The second Reptiloid grabbed the Warrior's left wrist.

Blade brought his right fist around and buried the knuckles in the mutant's mouth. Teeth shattered and greenish fluid spurted everywhere. Blade delivered another devastating punch, and the Reptiloid collapsed on the floor.

Gat was on his hand and knees, shaking his head to clear his benumbed mind.

The other two guards were scrambling to their feet.

Blade snap kicked his right boot into the face of the mutant in front of him. The Reptiloid actually became airborne, sailing into the opposite wall and toppling onto its stomach.

The last guard was erect, a pike in its left hand. With an enraged snarl, the Reptiloid speared the point at the Warrior.

Blade wrenched his body backwards, the pike missing his chin by inches. His right hand flicked out and gripped the shaft of the pike just below the sharp head and above the Reptiloid's left hand. He held onto the shaft, jerking the mutant up short, and planted his left boot on the guard's right knee.

The kneecap shattered with a pronounced snap and the Reptiloid began to buckle, stunned by the excruciating agony.

Blade fiercely yanked the pike from the guard's hand, then brought the pike down on top of the mutant's cranium.

With a groan, the final guard slumped to the floor.

Gat was almost upright and starting to lift his pike.

Blade closed in, swinging his pike like a club and catching Gat on the side of the head.

Gat staggered, green blood flowing from his wound.

Blade buried his right boot in the Reptiloid's crotch, and he was supremely gratified when Gat grunted and doubled over. Blade let the mutant have another boot to the chin.

Gat went down for the count.

Now which way should he go?

Blade paused, surveying the corridor in both directions. The hallway was deserted, but another Reptiloid could appear at any second and sound the alarm.

Where would he find the others?

Blade turned to the left and jogged in search of his companions. He wasn't leaving without the captured Force members. He'd die first!

A door materialized at the end of the corridor, a wooden door lacking a barred window.

Blade reached the door and opened it an inch, delighted to discover a stairwell on the other side leading downward. He threw the door wide and stepped onto a landing.

The stairs were wooden with a green metal railing. They seemed to descend into the bowels of the earth.

Blade scanned the landing, disappointed at not finding a door or window he could use to reach the outside. Either he used the stairwell or he returned along the corridor and risked being recaptured.

The shouting of agitated voices to his rear decided the issue.

Blade took the stairs two at a time as he hastened below. He needed somewhere to hide until the heat was off. But where? He came to another landing and continued lower. How many floors had Prine said the Imperium contained? Ten? Plus the Arena, whatever that was. There should be plenty of hiding places in such a vast structure.

If only he wouldn't run into more Reptiloids!

He did.

Blade was three steps from the next landing when a pair of mutants unexpectedly appeared, coming up the stairwell, talking quietly.

The Warrior and the Reptiloids reached the landing simultaneously.

Blade never broke his stride. He attacked, striking right and left with the pike.

Initially startled by the sudden onslaught of the giant, the Reptiloids reacted adroitly, separating to catch him in a pincer movement. Both toted pikes, and one of them, it turned out, was an expert at wielding the weapon.

Blade dispatched the first mutant, the Reptiloid on his left, with a minimum of fuss. He missed his rushing swing, sidestepped a counterthrust, and speared his pike into the lizard-man's throat.

Gurgling and clutching at its ruptured neck, the Reptiloid staggered backwards and fell onto the landing.

Blade spun to confront the second Reptiloid.

This one was holding his pike at chest height and regarding the giant with a calculating eye. "You are the one I've heard about," he said calmly. "The big human who killed three of my kind."

Blade nodded.

The Reptiloid smiled. "I will teach you a lesson you will never forget, human swine!"

"This year or next?" Blade retorted.

The Reptiloid closed on the Warrior, deftly handling the pike with consummate skill.

Blade blocked the flurry of stabs and thrusts, realizing he was up against a master. Only his power and speed enabled him to ward off the mutant's early assault. He was forced to retreat over a yard, and once the Reptiloid's pike nicked his left cheek.

The mutant abruptly stepped back and appraised the Warrior. "I understand now. No other human has ever lasted even this long."

"Why?" Blade responded. "Do you only pick on children?"

"For that," the Reptiloid stated, hefting his pike, "you will die a slow death."

"Anything would be better than listening to you flap your gums," Blade said, scrunching up his nose. "And you really should do something about your breath!"

With a snarl, the mutant tried to impale the giant's groin.

Blade narrowly avoided the blow. As a lifelong admirer of edged weaponry, he had spent many an hour in the enormous Family library perusing every book he could find on the subject. Volumes on knives had fascinated him from an early age. Ancient warfare books were also a special interest. The Founder had stocked over a dozen books on Rome and Greece. One of them, in particular, was devoted to a scholarly discussion of the Roman military machinery. The Roman soldiers had utilized a variety of weapons, but chief among them was the pike. And the Roman pike, according to the material Blade had read, corresponded in every respect to the type used by the Reptiloids. Both versions were simply heavy, formidable javelins, effective when thrown at a distance and decidedly deadly at close range. All of these thoughts flitted through the Warrior's mind as he swiftly backpedaled to evade a second sweep of the mutant's pike. At a range of only three yards the Reptiloid would likely be expecting him to fight by applying the stab-and-thrust techniques normally employed at such a short distance. But what if he reversed the tactics? What if he *threw* his pike instead?

Hissing angrily, the Reptiloid lunged, his pike held straight out from his waist.

Blade artfully ducked to the right, his steely right arm bringing his pike up and around in the traditional overhand spear toss.

The Reptiloid attempted to dodge to the left, but at a span of three yards there wasn't enough time to react. The glittering tip of the Warrior's pike penetrated the mutant's chest, passing through the lizard-man's body and projecting out his back. The Reptiloid stumbled sideways and collided with the landing wall, its eyes blinking at a fast clip, its mouth wide. Gasping for air, the mutant gazed at the giant in astonishment, then died, sliding down the wall and pitching onto the floor.

Blade scooped up the pike of the first Reptiloid he'd slain. He hurried down the stairs, wondering how much time he had before the Reptiloids on the upper level deduced he was in the stairwell.

A commotion at the top of the stairs served as his answer.

He was out of time!

Blade came to the next landing and angled toward a door to his right. Every landing below the upper level had doors, undoubtedly affording access to the inner passages of the Imperium.

Where would this one lead?

He yanked the door open and walked into a plush corridor complete with red carpet, paneled walls, and lanterns attached to gold fixtures on those walls.

The Reptiloids would find the pair on the landing at any moment!

He had to discover a hiding place, and quick!

Blade jogged along the hall, seeking a door, another stairwell, anything. After traveling 25 yards, he saw a door to his right. Throwing caution to the wind, he twisted the knob and stepped boldly inside.

And immediately regretted his rashness.

The chamber in front of him was huge, its spaciousness enhanced by a vaulted crystal ceiling. In the center reared an imposing marble throne perched on a circular series of gold encrusted steps. Reptiloids were everywhere. Between the doorway and the throne stood four dozen lizard-men, two dozen on either side, forming a living aisle to the throne. They were standing at attention, their pikes at their sides. All eyes were on the Warrior.

Blade frowned, exasperated at his stupidity. His gaze alighted on the regal throne as a stately voice rang out.

"Come in, Blade! I've been expecting you! But kindly drop that pike you're holding, or my personal guard will be constrained to use you for a pincushion!"

Blade released the pike and it fell to the soft, red carpet.

A towering figure stirred on the throne.

"I believe you have been eager to meet me," the figure declared, rising. "I know I have been eager to meet you. I've heard a lot about you, Warrior. My name is Reptilian."

PART FOUR
OF REPTILIAN AND MEN

CHAPTER TWELVE

"One of us should talk to him."

"You talk to him, Boone," Sergeant Havoc snapped. "If it was up to me, I'd kill the son of a bitch with my bare hands."

"He didn't know," Boone said.

Sergeant Havoc glared to his right, his lips tightening at the sight of the Clansman huddled in the far corner of the room. "That's no excuse! I'll never forgive him for what he did! Those men were friends of mine!"

Thunder, his arms crossed over his chest, gazed at Kraft. "Put yourself in his shoes. Imagine how he must feel."

"He brought it on himself!" Sergeant Havoc stated. "He can suffer the consequences by himself!" He turned and tramped to the door, staring through the window at the six mutants in the corridor.

Boone looked at the noncom's back. "Nothing we can say will make Havoc change his mind." He sighed. "And I can't say as I blame him."

"Then one of us must talk to Kraft," Thunder said. "As much as we dislike him, we are all on the same team, all part of the same unit. How many times has Blade told us we must stick together at all costs?"

"Blade wasn't here to see what Kraft did," Boone noted.

"Will you go, or should I?" Thunder inquired bluntly.

Boone reflected for a bit. "I'll do it," he offered.

"Are you certain?" Thunder queried. "I don't mind being the one."

Boone glanced in the direction of the despondent Clansman. "No. I'll do it. I've always been a glutton for punishment." He stared at the cot, at the putrid pile next to the cot. "I wish they'd clean up that mess! It reeks!"

"These creatures have no compassion," Thunder commented. "They are a violation of the natural order. They are an abomination to the Spirit-In-All-Things."

"Not only that," Boone said. "They're just plain ugly." He walked toward Kraft, thoughtfully chewing on his lower lip. The Clansman had withdrawn into himself after the incident with the burgers. Kraft had not uttered a word since. He simply sat there, his knees tucked against his chest, his arms around his legs, with his chin on his knees and a blank expression on his face. The man was obviously in shock. What can I say, Boone asked himself, to snap Kraft out of it? How do you deal with abject depression?

Kraft never bothered to look up as the Cavalryman approached.

Boone halted a few feet away. "Kraft?"

Kraft didn't budge.

Boone moved closer and squatted alongside the man in leather. "Kraft? It's me. Boone."

There wasn't the faintest hint of a reaction.

"Talk to me, Kraft," Boone urged.

Kraft said nothing.

Boone pursed his lips, studying the Clansman. Now what should he do? Slap Kraft a couple of times? "Kraft. Talk to me. I want to help," Boone said, scarcely believing he was saying the words. The last person in the world he would ever want to help was Kraft. Of all the people Boone had ever known, and he had known some real bastards, Kraft was the most obnoxious. "Is there anything I can do for you?"

The Clansman might as well have been chiseled from stone.

Boone extended his right arm and placed his hand on Kraft's left shoulder. "Kraft?"

The Clansman's lips moved, feebly mouthing a word.

Boone leaned forward. "What was that? I didn't catch it?"

Kraft repeated the word, his voice barely above a whisper. "Don't," he said.

"Don't? Don't what?" Boone inquired.

"Don't touch me," Kraft stated bleakly.

Boone withdrew his right hand. "Whatever you want. Would you like to talk?"

"Leave me alone," Kraft mumbled.

"I need to talk to you," Boone insisted.

"No," Kraft said.

"Yep," Boone countered. "You've got to snap out of this."

"Go away," Kraft murmured.

"I can't," Boone said. "We need you on your feet when we

make our break. We're going to try and jump these things if they ever come in, and we're not leaving without you."

"Leave me," Kraft said. "Who cares what happens to me?"

"Don't you?" Boone queried.

"Nope," Kraft replied sincerely.

"Why?"

Kraft's eyes finally blinked, moistening as he inhaled deeply and looked at Boone. "Don't ask stupid questions."

"You can't let it get to you," Boone stated. "Not now."

"I . . . I . . ." Kraft began, but he was unable to complete his sentence.

"Let it out," Boone suggested. "Get it off your chest."

"Why should you care?" Kraft declared testily.

"We're all part of the Force," Boone said. "We must help each other."

Kraft's shoulders slumped and he closed his eyes. "I . . . I didn't mean to do it," he said weakly.

"I know," Boone said.

"I just wanted to feed my face."

"I know," Boone reiterated.

Kraft groaned. "You have no idea how I feel. It's like I'm dead inside. I did the worst thing you could ever possibly do." He paused. "I *ate* someone else!"

"You were tricked," Boone observed. "You didn't know what you were doing."

Kraft didn't respond.

Boone frowned. This was getting him nowhere. They would need all the help they could get when they jumped the mutants. Kraft had to come around.

But how to do it?

"Suit yourself," Boone said, shrugging. "If you want to sit here and mope, that's your business. I just thought you might want to get even with Gat and his buddies."

Kraft opened his eyes. "Get even?"

"Sure," Boone stated. "You don't think we're going to take all of this lying down, do you?"

"How can we get even?" Kraft inquired.

"By doing as much damage as we can," Boone said. "They must have our weapons and backpacks around here somewhere. If we can get our hands on them, we'll show these jackasses a thing or two."

Kraft's eyes narrowed. "I would like to rack that prick Gat."

"You may get the chance," Boone commented. "But you must get your act together if you're coming with us."

Kraft's mouth compressed into a thin line as he wrestled with his emotions.

"We know Blade is here," Boone added. "We must hitch up with him and do a number on these mutants."

"What chance do we stand against all those freaks?" Kraft asked.

"What chance do we have if we do nothing?" Boone rejoined. "I doubt they'll let any of us live, and if they do we'll live as slaves. I'm not too fond of that notion."

"I'll never be their slave!" Kraft vowed. His complexion was slowly returning to normal.

"You're with us then?" Boone queried.

Kraft nodded. "I'm with you."

"Good. Come with me." Boone stood and ambled over to Thunder. "Now all we need is for them to open that door."

Thunder smiled at Kraft. "I am happy you have recovered."

"I'll never recover," Kraft said brusquely, then softened his tone. "But thanks."

Boone looked toward the door. "What's happening out there?"

"Nothing much," Sergeant Havoc replied. "The pissants are standing around shooting the breeze."

"Maybe we can outfox them," Boone proposed.

"How?" Thunder asked.

"Let's plan this together," Boone proposed. "Havoc!" he called out. "We need you."

Sergeant Havoc walked toward them, his flinty blue eyes riveted on Kraft.

Kraft averted his face.

"What is it?" Havoc asked.

"We need an idea to draw those mutants in here," Boone stated. "Once they're inside, we'll jump them."

"There are a half dozen out there right now," Sergeant Havoc divulged. "We'll be outnumbered, and they have pikes while we're unarmed."

"Does this mean you don't want to try and escape," Boone inquired.

"I was just noting the odds," Havoc said. "I'm with you one hundred percent."

"Then how do we draw them in here?" Boone asked. "Pretend one of us is sick?"

"That's the oldest trick in the book," Sergeant Havoc commented. "And they may not care if one of us is sick. We need something else."

"I have a suggestion," Thunder spoke up.

"What?" Boone inquired.

"The creature called Gat said we must keep our strength up for the arena," Thunder reminded them. "They are saving us for a special fate. If so, they would not want us to harm one another."

"You think we should stage a fight?" Boone deduced.

Thunder shrugged. "Unless one of you has a better alternative."

"But who should do the fighting?" Boone questioned. "You and I?"

"If you want the fight to be as realistic as possible," Sergeant Havoc said, "Kraft and I will go at it."

Kraft's head snapped up. "What?"

"I don't know. . . ." Boone stated uncertainly.

"A fight is a great idea," Havoc persisted. "Kraft and I will put on a good show and lure the guards in here."

"You and me?" Kraft said reservedly.

"Sure. Why not?" Havoc rejoined. "You aren't afraid, are you?"

"I ain't afraid of you!" Kraft snapped.

Havoc smiled and stepped to the center of the cell. "Prove it."

Boone clutched Kraft's right arm. "You don't have to do this if you don't want to. I'll square off against Havoc."

Kraft gazed at the noncom. "No. I'll do it." He walked toward the trooper.

Boone hesitated, reluctant to see the pair clash, worried their mock combat would turn into the real McCoy.

Thunder moved in the direction of the cell door. "Come on," he urged the frontiersman.

Boone, frowning, complied. He took a position at the small window with Thunder to his left. Together they looked at the duo in the middle of the room.

Sergeant Havoc adopted the Zenkutsu-tachi, the forward stance, with his fists clenched in the Oriental fashion. His thumbs were bent over the second joints of his first two fingers, instead of on the side of the fist as was the Western style. He grinned at the Clansman. "I'm ready when you are."

"This isn't fair," Kraft said. "You'll break every bone in my body."

"Not every bone," Havoc stated. "Just the major ones."

Boone glanced out the window. The six mutants were engaged in idle conversation. Three of them held pikes. The rest had leaned their pikes against the wall. He looked back at Havoc and Kraft. "Let's get this show on the road."

Sergeant Havoc grinned and snap-kicked his right foot at Kraft's face.

Kraft sidestepped to the left and assumed an uneven horse stance. He swung his left fist at the noncom's chin.

Sergeant Havoc easily evaded the blow, dodging to the right and countering with a spin kick. His right heel slammed into the Clansman's abdomen and doubled Kraft over.

Watching from the door, Boone decided the time was ripe. He raised his right hand and pounded on the glass. "Hey! Open up! There's a fight in here!"

The lizard-men gazed at the cell door, but none of them made a move toward it.

Come on! Boone's mind screamed.

Sergeant Havoc brought his hands around and in, boxing Kraft on the ears with the heels of his palms.

"In here!" Boone cried. "There's a fight!"

One of the mutants came up to the door.

Boone stepped aside and waved his left hand toward the center of the room where Sergeant Havoc was just delivering his right knee to the point of Kraft's chin.

The lizard-man took one look and reached for the bolt.

"Here they come!" Boone whispered to Thunder, who promptly flattened against the wall adjacent to the door's inner edge.

Kraft was on his knees with Sergeant Havoc standing over him.

The door swung out and three of the lizard-men entered, two of them with their pikes.

"You there!" the mutant in the lead shouted. "Stop fighting!"

Sergeant Havoc ignored the command. Instead, he kicked Kraft in the stomach and the Clansman went down.

"Didn't you hear me?" the lead mutant yelled. "Stop fighting this instant!" He headed for Havoc and Kraft, his two companions right behind him.

Boone stared at the doorway.

Where were the other three? They needed all six in the cell if their plan was to succeed.

The remaining trio walked into the room, all three bearing their pikes. They strode forward.

And Boone initiated the bedlam by stepping in close to the nearest lizard-man and hooking his left leg under the mutant's legs, catching the creature from the rear. The lizard-man toppled backwards, its arms swinging wildly in a vain effort to stay erect, its pike in its left hand. Boone snatched at the weapon, and to his amazement it came loose from the mutant's grip.

A second lizard-man caught the frontiersman's attack out of the corner of its left eye. It spun, leveling its pike.

Thunder vaulted from behind the door, tackling the second mutant around the waist and they both sprawled onto the floor.

With a deft flip of his wrists, Boone reversed the pike and plunged the razor tip into the first mutant's left eye.

The cell became a whirlwind of conflict as the Force members fought for their freedom.

Sergeant Havoc closed on the three mutants in the lead, executing a spectacular Yoko-tobi-geri, a side jump kick, and ramming his right boot into the head guard's face, bowling the mutant over.

Thunder and the lizard-man he'd tackled were wrestling on the floor.

Boone wrenched the pike from the dead mutant's eye socket and pivoted to confront two of the creatures coming at him with their pikes extended.

"Enough!" a familiar voice abruptly bellowed. "Cease this nonsense immediately!"

All action froze as all eyes, human and mutant, shifted to the doorway.

Gat stood there, his pike in his right hand, rage on his face. "Drop that pike!" he ordered, his lips split and puffy.

Boone balked at relinquishing the weapon.

Gat stepped to the right of the door and motioned toward the doorway. "Drop it or die!" His left ear was swollen and discolored.

Boone's eyes widened at the sight of two dozen mutants lined up in the corridor, each one armed with a pike.

"We came to escort you to the Arena," Gat declared. "But none of you will reach the Arena alive if you don't do exactly as I say. Now drop the damn pike!"

Reluctantly, Boone let go and the weapon clattered on the cement floor.

Gat gazed at the dead lizard-man. "You humans are more trouble than you're worth! I can't wait to see you torn apart in the Arena!" He looked at each Force member in turn, sheer fury radiating from his features. "Prepare to die, you miserable slime!"

CHAPTER THIRTEEN

Reptilian was an awesome mutant. He possessed the characteristic traits of his kind, the same dark green skin, the same elongated nose, the same round ears, and the same set of pointed teeth. But he stood a foot taller than the average Reptiloid, and his bodily proportions matched Blade's in every respect. Reptilian's eyes were a deep, eerie blue, animated by his devious genius intellect. Unlike the other male Reptiloids, who all wore a standard garment consisting of a pair of green pants, Reptilian adorned his person in a striking red outfit: a red shirt, red pants, red boots, and even a red cape. He smiled at the Warrior and beckoned with his right arm. "Come here. We have much to discuss."

Blade gazed at the mutants packing the throne room, his eyes narrowing at the sight of the first female Reptiloids he had seen. They were counterparts of the males in every respect, except their breasts, naturally, were considerably larger. The females wore green garments covering them from their ankles to their necks. He wondered why the Reptiloids preferred to wear green? Was it because the color matched their skin and afforded an excellent camouflage when they were on the surface?

Reptilian noticed the Warrior's scrutiny of the chamber and misconstrued the reason. "Don't worry," he declared. "None of my followers will harm you here. You have my word on it, and the word of Reptilian is inviolate."

Blade walked toward the throne, his skin tingling as he moved between the two rows of Reptilian's personal guard. He halted at the base of the golden stairs and looked up at the mutant leader.

Reptilian studied the Warrior for a moment, then smiled. "You are perfect."

"Perfect for what?" Blade asked.

Reptilian ignored the question. He sat down on his marble throne and motioned for Blade to ascend the steps. "Don't be shy. We have much to discuss," he reiterated.

Blade slowly climbed the stairs until he stood on the top level next to the throne. "What do we have to talk about?"

"I want to know all about you," Reptilian said.

"Why?"

Again Reptilian disregarded the Warrior's query. "I can see we have a lot in common," he commented.

"How do you figure that?" Blade remarked.

Reptilian rested his chin in his right hand. "You, obviously, are a giant among your kind. I, by the same token, am a giant among mine. We should thank our parents for the exceptional genes they bestowed upon us."

"My parents have already passed on to the higher mansions," Blade said.

"The higher mansions?" Reptilian repeated quizzically. "Don't tell me you believe in an afterlife?"

Blade recalled the teachings he had received from the Family Elders. "The afterlife is merely a continuation of this life," he stated. "If you have the faintest flicker of faith, then you never really die."

"This life is all we get," Reptilian disagreed. "There is no afterlife. Only simpletons believe that old wives' tale."

"I believe it," Blade asserted. "And there are dozens more like me where I come from."

"Is it true you come from Minnesota?" Reptilian asked.

Blade didn't answer.

Reptilian shrugged. "Suit yourself. But I already know everything of importance about you."

"Sure you do," Blade said sarcastically.

"I know you are the leader of the elite unit known as the Force," Reptilian said. "I know you were sent here to terminate me." He chuckled. "And I know you will singularly fail."

"I haven't failed," Blade said.

Reptilian encompassed the chamber in an expensive gesture. "No? Then what would you call this?"

"Planning my strategy," Blade commented.

Reptilian laughed. "I like you. A sense of humor is essential."

"You're not what I expected," Blade mentioned.

Reptilian cocked his head to the left. "Oh? What did you expect? An ogre with one eye and ten legs?"

"Something like that," Blade admitted.

"You humans are so predictable!" Reptilian declared. "If a species is different from yours, you automatically assume it is inferior."

"You're a fine one to talk," Blade countered. "I've heard about the way you treat humans, as slaves and food."

"Humans are mindless cattle," Reptilian declared. "I treat them the way they should be treated."

"Humans and mutants can be friends, you know," Blade noted.

"Friends?" Reptilian snapped, straightening. "You appear to be laboring under a severe misconception! Humans and mutants can never be friends for the simple reason humans can never be trusted!"

"That's ridiculous," Blade said.

"Is it?" Reptilian responded angrily. "Sixty years ago I tried to befriend your species, but they would have none of it! Instead they tried to kill me! And why? Just because I was different!" He scowled. "The irony of it all! I am different from your kind because your kind unleashed a holocaust of global dimensions and contaminated the environment with radioactive and chemical warfare toxins. I am different from your kind because massive doses of radiation drastically alter embryonic formation and development. And if the subsequent mutations mature and breed, they pass on their genetic traits to their offspring. The mutated strain continues to evolve over generations, becoming increasingly mutant with each one."

"I've never heard that theory before," Blade commented.

"It is not a theory," Reptilian stated. "It is an established fact. Permit me to elaborate. One hundred and five years ago, at the outset of World War Three, my ancestors were fully human. They lived near San Diego, which sustained a direct nuclear hit during the war. Although they were outside of the blast radius, they must have been exposed to the fallout, to the radiation. They migrated northward shortly thereafter, and about ten years later they had a child, a boy. This son was not quite human, nor was he completely mutated. He had pale green skin and red pupils, but his features were typical of your species. Over the span of decades, with each generation, his children, and then his children's children, and his children's children's children, all became increasingly mutant." He smiled. "You see the end result before you."

"All of which reinforces my point," Blade said. "If your lineage was once human, then your species shares the same ancestors. We should be able to share as equals and friends."

Reptilian pursed his thin lips and scrutinized the Warrior. "You truly believe that, don't you?"

"Of course," Blade replied. "At my Home humans and mutants live in harmony. You could do the same here."

"Not true," Reptilian said. "There may be a few exceptions to the general rule, but humans and mutants are destined to be implacable enemies. As a species we can never be friends because your kind will not permit us to attain our rightful destiny."

"Which is?" Blade asked.

"Why, to dominate the world, of course," Reptilian said sincerely. "The mutant species developed as a consequence of humankind's abysmal failure to manage this planet with wisdom and insight. Let's face facts. Your kind blew it. You had the opportunity to utilize the planetary resources to maximize peace and prosperity for all, but you weren't up to the task. You destroyed your civilization and you have only yourselves to blame." He paused. "The Mutant Era will be different."

"The Mutant Era?"

"Yes," Reptilian said, grinning. "The era of the ascendancy of my species over yours. The New Order I've established will eventually supplant the human species as the dominant species on this world."

"What is this New Order?" Blade inquired.

"The Province is not the only organized pocket of mutantkind," Reptilian disclosed. "And I am not the only leader of a budding mutant autocracy. I have sent out scouts and located other mutant outposts. Slowly but surely I am forming a mutant empire which will supplant the crumbling vestiges of human culture. Within another century we shall rule this globe."

"Don't hold your breath," Blade quipped.

"Mark my words," Reptilian insisted. "Mutants will one day subjugate humanity. We are the wave of the future."

"So how many other mutant outposts are in the New Order?" Blade casually inquired.

Reptilian grinned. "Nice try. Such information is confidential, you understand. Although you may be privileged to see the leaders of the New Order during the Arena festivities."

"Lucky me," Blade cracked.

Reptilian paid no attention. "The leaders of the New Order gather for periodic conclaves. They like to attend during Arena week. Every two months or so we like to put on a special entertainment in the Arena."

"What kind of entertainment?" Blade inquired.

"Can you read?" Reptilian unexpectedly questioned.

Blade's forehead furrowed. "Yes. Everyone in my Family can."

"I'm impressed," Reptilian said. "Reading is a lost art outside of the civilized territories and outposts. I encourage my subjects to learn to read at an early age. We teach the young Reptiloids to read by the age of five."

"What does all of this have to do with the entertainment in your Arena?" Blade asked.

"Everything," Reptilian responded. "When I was forming the Province, I researched all the ancient texts I could find on various types of government. I wanted to find the ideal form." He gestured at the royal chamber. "And I found it. Ancient Rome. I've patterned the Province after the Roman system of government. I've named our headquarters, our palace if you will, the Imperium. And, in keeping with the Roman style of entertainment, I had an Arena built."

Blade remembered reading about the Roman stadiums and the barbaric contests the Romans had sanctioned. The individual fighters had been known as gladiators. He recalled specific historical accounts; gladiators had been forced to battle starved lions, or a group of gladiators had fought against a pack of panthers. The Romans had delighted in having their gladiators fight with mismatched weapons. Such sickening cruelty had been exalted as the highest form of entertainment. "Do you have gladiators in your Arena?" he queried.

"Of what use is an Arena without gladiators?" Reptilian answered.

"Will I be one of these gladiators?" Blade asked bluntly.

"No," Reptilian said. "I have other plans for you. I will not run the risk of having you injured in combat."

"Why are you being so kind to me?" Blade asked with a tinge of derision.

"I will explain," Reptilian said, "in due time. First, though, I would like you to attend the Arena with me as my official guest."

"Don't you mean your official prisoner?" Blade corrected the mutant.

Reptilian slowly rose, his cape swirling to his knees. "I am doing my best to treat you with civility. The least you could do is reciprocate."

"You must be joking," Blade said.

Reptilian stared at the captive. "Your species has no class."

"You have no room to talk," Blade responded. "And I'm not going anywhere with you until you answer a few questions of mine."

"Why don't we talk while we walk?" Reptilian proposed, starting to descend the stairs.

"Now," Blade snapped.

Reptilian sighed. "Very well. What is bothering you?"

"Where is the rest of the Force?" Blade asked.

"You will see them at the Arena," Reptilian stated.

"I will?" Blade queried in disbelief.

"I have given my word," Reptilian said stiffly. "You will see some of them, anyway."

"Which ones? What happened to the rest?" Blade pressed him.

Reptilian resumed his descent. "If you want answers, you must come with me. If you don't want to attend the Arena, I will have you returned to your cell."

Blade realized he didn't have a choice. He wanted to see Boone and the others, to find out what was happening to them. "I'll come," he said.

Reptilian looked up, smirking. "How nice. Shall we?" He waited for Blade to reach him before continuing down to the floor.

"You must have it pretty cushy here," Blade commented. "Setting yourself up as a king and all."

"Not a king," Reptilian said. "An emperor. There is a fine distinction."

"Either way you cut it," Blade observed, "you're a dictator."

Reptilian grinned. "True. But I deserve to be a dictator."

"Why's that?"

They began moving toward the door, walking between the rows of guards.

"Greatness is inherently mine by virtue of my biological preeminence," Reptilian asserted.

Blade glanced at the lizard-man. "You must wear out a lot of mirrors."

Reptilian paused. "Mirrors?"

"Yeah," Blade said. "From kissing your reflection all the time."

Surprisingly, Reptilian threw back his head and laughed. "I must remember that line. Gat will appreciate it."

"Where is Gat?" Blade asked as they kept going to the door.

"He will meet us there," Reptilian said.

The Reptiloids in the chamber were conversing in a routine manner. They did not display any undue interest in Reptilian's Arena guest.

Blade was feeling increasingly apprehensive. Reptilian was being too nice, and there had to be an ulterior motive. But what? Why was Reptilian taking him to the Arena? What was the mutant leader up to?

Reptilian opened the door and nodded for Blade to proceed. Together they strolled to the stairwell with Reptilian's personal guard right behind them.

As they entered the stairwell Blade looked up. Were the pair he'd slain still up there? Or had the Reptiloids taken the bodies away? What would Reptilian do when he learned about their deaths?

"The two you killed on the landing above us have been taken to the crematorium," Reptilian mentioned offhandedly.

Blade glanced at the mutant. "Are you a mind reader?"

Reptilian chuckled. "Nothing so profound. I used deductive reasoning and prior knowledge. I knew you had killed two of my subjects on one of the landings above us, and when I saw you staring upward I guessed your train of thought."

"How did you know I killed them?" Blade asked. "And how did you know I'd escaped from my cell? When you first saw me, you claimed you'd been expecting me."

Reptilian reached up and tapped the right side of his head. "Deductive reasoning again. I was informed of your escape within

a minute of its occurrence, and I was told about the landing
incident seconds before you blundered into the throne room."

"You were informed? How?" Blade wanted to learn.

Reptilian slid his right hand around his back, under his cape. His
hand emerged holding a small, square, black plastic device with
dials and a little speaker on the front and a belt clip on the reverse.
"These were once known as walkie-talkies. With the generator
we obtained, and with our supply of rechargeable batteries, we
find these walkie-talkies are ideal for communicating at distances
up to a mile."

Blade knew about walkie-talkies; they were commonly used by
the California military. "Where did you get your walkie-talkies
and all the rest?"

"Where else? The black market. The Scarlet Clique does
business with anyone, mutant or human," Reptilian divulged.
"But then, you probably know all about the Scarlet Clique.
Everyone does business with them."

Blade had never heard of the Scarlet Clique before, but he
wasn't about to reveal his ignorance. "I imagine everyone does,"
he commented.

"They're the best supplier I know of," Reptilian said. He
reattached the walkie-talkie to the back of his belt, then proceeded
down the stairwell.

Blade stayed alongside the mutant. "Where do you suppose
they obtain all the equipment and other items they supply?"

Reptilian shrugged. "I've never asked. Such a breach of
etiquette would be unforgivable. If I foolishly pried into their
affairs, they would sever our business relationship. And I need the
merchandise they can provide." He paused. "I suspect they steal
most of their goods from the Russians, the Civilized Zone, and
California. Their network of thieves spans the country. I've even
heard rumors it's international in scope."

An international ring of thieves? Black marketeering on a grand
scale? This was information the Freedom Federation would
consider crucial. How could he pump Reptilian without arousing
the Reptiloid's suspicions? "I've heard the same rumors," he lied.

"You have?" Reptilian said. "You're the fourth one to tell me
that. The rumors must have a basis in fact."

"Who do you think runs the Scarlet Clique?" Blade inquired.

"I don't know," Reptilian replied. "Trying to discover the identity of the head of the Scarlet Clique would be hazardous to your health."

Blade pondered for a moment. What else could he ask without giving himself away? "They like their secrecy, don't they?"

"Can you blame them? They work both sides of the fence, and they do so without stepping on anyone's toes. Their transactions are conducted in the utmost secrecy. To tell you the truth, I envy their superb organizational skills." Reptilian gazed over the railing toward the bottom. "We are almost there."

"Do you mind if I ask you a question?" Blade queried, recalling his conversation with the Indoctrinator, Prine.

"I may not answer it," Reptilian said.

"I know," Blade stated. "But I've been wondering about something. When your Hunter Squad fought with us in the forest, they seemed to be able to spot us even when we were concealed. And when Prime was talking to me, he claimed the Reptiloids have some sort of heat-detecting ability. Do you?"

"Yes," Reptilian confirmed. "Our vision is slightly better than human sight. I believe our range is extended further into the infrared spectrum than yours is. Have you ever seen a road on a hot day? Have you seen the heat reflecting off the road surface in seemingly wavy lines?"

"Yes," Blade said.

"Our vision works on the same principle," Reptilian explained. "Every body gives off a degree of heat. Mammals gives off more than reptiles, reptiles more than fish, and so on. Our vision enables us to see the heat being radiated by a physical form. If you were hiding behind a boulder, for instance, and even if I didn't actually see your body, I would be able to detect your presence by the heat your body was radiating. Our vision is not infallible. We can't see through solid objects, and on cold days physical forms give off less heat, which means they're harder to discern. But our ability is particularly beneficial when we are engaged in combat in rough terrain, as you discovered. We enjoy a decided advantage."

"I'll say," Blade agreed.

They came to the lowest landing. There was only one door, to the right.

"Prepare yourself," Reptilian said as he took hold of the door handle. "You have never beheld a sight like my Arena!" he boasted proudly.

Beyond the door was a long corridor painted entirely in red. They walked along it for hundreds of yards. In the distance a blue door became visible.

"What's that noise?" Blade inquired as a muted jumble of sound reached his ears.

"You will see," Reptilian responded, grinning.

The sound grew in volume, becoming a steady din.

Blade glanced over his right shoulder at the escort of personal guards. Their faces were impassive as they marched with their pikes aligned on their right shoulders in practiced military precision.

A thunderous roar shook the corridor.

Blade looked at Reptilian.

The mutant laughed. "One of my pets."

"What is it? A dinosaur?" Blade quipped.

"Close," Reptilian said. They walked to the blue door and he grabbed the knob. "There is nothing like the Arena. The Romans had the right idea all along." So saying, he turned the knob and pulled. "After you."

Blade stepped through the doorway, his gray eyes widening in amazement at the scene before him. "Incredible!" he declared.

"Thank you," Reptilian said from behind him.

The Arena was every bit as awe-inspriing as the Reptiloid leader had claimed. One hundred yards in length and 30 yards wide, the stadium was patterned after the Roman amphitheaters of old. The Arena floor was mere dirt, and countless dark splotches dotting the soil served as a silent testimony to the numerous lives lost during the games. A ten-foot wooden wall separated the spectators from the contestants. Rings of seats rose from the top of the wall in successively elevated tiers. The ceiling consisted of a latticework of huge beams braced by massive marble columns positioned around the outer row of seats. Over a dozen large doors were situated at regular intervals in the inner wall, affording access to the Arena floor.

Reptilian stepped up to Blade's left side. "Initially, I intended to construct an Arena only half this size. But when we were excavating for the Imperium, we found an enormous cavern adjacent to the Rogue River, under what was once Riverside Park. I decided the cavern would be perfect for the Arena."

Blade was surveying the stands, boggled by the sight of thousands of spectators. The Reptiloids occupied the rows nearest the Arena floor, the best seats for viewing the action. Blade estimated at least a thousand mutants were in attendance, but there were even more humans. They filled in the seats above the Reptiloids, and they were closely monitored by guards posted every few rows. The conversation of thousands of voices accounted for the racket he had heard in the corridor.

"Arena days are special," Reptilian mentioned. "Almost the entire population of the Province is here."

"You allow your human slaves to attend?" Blade asked.

"This is the only diversion they're permitted," Reptilian said. "They look forward to the games."

Blade gazed upward, spying a series of gigantic floodlights affixed to the wooden beams. "Your generator supplies the power," he deduced.

"Yes," Reptilian verified.

Blade noted his immediate surroundings for the first time. He was on a spacious platform located at the top of the inner wall directly above one of the doors. A half-dozen plush red chairs were lined up near the edge of the platform nearest the combat area.

"Watch this," Reptilian said, and walked out to the platform's rim.

The audience went wild, cheering and applauding. Chants of "Reptilian! Reptilian! Reptilian!" arose from the stands.

Blade was astonished to see the human spectators participating in the ovation. Why would the humans respond so enthusiastically? Had they been conditioned by the Reptiloids? Would they suffer a dire fate if they didn't applaud?

Reptilian was basking in the acclamation, his arms upraised, beaming. He turned and motioned for the Warrior to join him.

Blade slowly moved to the leader's right. He looked back and saw the personal guards filing from the corridor, one line branching to the right, the other to the left. They enclosed the platform on three sides, a living phalanx of protection for Reptilian.

"Reptilian! Reptilian!" the crowd shouted adoringly.

Blade glanced to his right, surprised to find a smaller platform twenty yards away. Seven chairs had been placed close to the lip of the wall, and in each chair sat a different mutant. These mutants were not Reptiloids; they were a diverse assortment of genetic deviates, each attired in splendid clothing. One was some sort of froglike man with bulging eyes and thick lips. Another resembled a cross between a bear and a human. The rest were a bizarre amalgam of traits, hideous creatures with alien aspects. Were they the leaders of the New Order? If so, why did they occupy a separate, smaller platform? Were they subservient in status to Reptilian? Was he the supreme mastermind behind the establishment of the Mutant Era?

"We should sit down," Reptilian directed, taking the centermost chair.

Blade complied. "Why are we the only ones on this platform?" he inquired, yelling to make himself heard above the crowd.

"Sometimes I invite guests to share the royal dais. Today, you have the honor," Reptilian said.

Blade nodded at the smaller platform. "What about them?"

"They are where they deserve to be," Reptilian stated brusquely.

"So much for mutant equality," Blade baited the Reptiloid.

Reptilian gazed at Blade with a condescending air. "I have no equals. Lesser mutants share equality."

"Now I know why you don't wear a hat," Blade taunted.

"A hat?" Reptilian repeated, puzzled. He reflected for a moment, then burst out laughing. "You really do have an excellent sense of humor."

"I'm sorry you took it so nicely," Blade cracked.

Reptilian faced the Arena. He raised his right arm, palm outward, and every voice was stilled. "Citizens of the Province!" he called out. "Another week of Arena festivities are upon us! The entertainment will be the best you have ever beheld! All human workers are hereby granted an executive leave of absence from toil until the games are concluded!"

The humans went wild, clapping appreciatively.

They certainly are well trained! Blade thought to himself. How could Reptilian exert such absolute control? Was his reign of terror that effective? How could the human population of the Province tolerate their enslavement? Especially when they knew they might be consumed without warning? Why did . . .

Hold it!

A striking inconsistency blossomed in his mind. "This doesn't make sense," he blurted.

Reptilian glanced at his guest. "What doesn't?"

"I was told there are two thousand humans in the Province," Blade said.

"More or less," Reptilian stated.

"And about twelve hundred Reptiloids," Blade mentioned.

"So?" Reptilian rejoined.

"So there aren't enough humans to suffice as a steady food supply for the Reptiloids," Blade said. "Not if each of you eats a human a day."

Reptilian laughed. "Where did you hear we eat a human a day?"

"I just assumed. . . ." Blade began.

Reptilian shook his head. "If we ate a human a day, our slaves would revolt en masse. Credit me with more intelligence than that! We consume a variety of foodstuffs, not just humans. Venison and elk meat figures prominently in our diet. They are our staples, along with fish. Human meat is a delicacy for us." He paused, scrutinizing the humans in the seats. "There are other factors involved. Our metabolism is not the same as yours. Humans must eat every day, but Reptiloids need only eat every three days. And the system I have established minimizes the stress on our human slaves."

"What system?"

Reptilian gazed at Blade and grinned slyly. "I will explain everything at the proper time. This is not it." He faced the Arena. "Let the games commence!"

A clamorous ovation greeted the announcement.

Blade stared at the Arena absently, speculating on what would be the first "entertainment" of the day. Lions against humans? Bears against women? Were there Reptiloid gladiators? Would the Reptiloids fight human "contestants"?

An answer was forthcoming when the door below the royal platform swung outward and four figures cautiously emerged.

Blade stiffened at the sight of the quartet. His hands gripped the arms of the chair until his knuckles were white. "No!" he exclaimed.

"Yes," Reptilian said calmly.

"Not them!" Blade stated.

But it was them: Boone, Thunder, Sergeant Havoc, and Kraft!

CHAPTER FOURTEEN

"It's Blade!" Boone cried as his gaze alighted on the platform.

The others swiveled toward the platform. They saw Blade rise from a red chair, his features contorted in rage, and take a step to the edge of the platform. The crowd started murmuring loudly.

"He's going to jump" Sergeant Havoc declared

The immense Reptiloid next to the Warrior suddenly lunged, grabbing Blade's left wrist and wrenching him backwards. Blade stumbled into his chair and toppled over backwards. Before he could regain his feet he was ringed by a dozen Reptiloids, their pikes pointed at his chest. The Reptiloid in the red outfit said a few words to the Warrior, then barked a command at the row of guards to his left.

"What's going on?" Kraft asked.

Ten guards marched onto the platform and took up positions above the Force members. They hoisted their pikes and assumed a throwing stance.

Blade was on his knees, livid. He yelled something to the Reptiloid in red.

"What did he say?" Kraft queried anxiously. "I didn't hear him." The audience was growing louder and louder.

"I did not catch every word," Thunder said. "But I gather Blade intended to join us. The big one in red stopped him and threatened to have us speared by the guards if Blade tries it again."

"Who is that freak in the red threads?" Kraft questioned.

"My guess is it's the leader of the Reptiloids," Boone commented. "The one they call Reptilian."

"I wish I had my switchblade," Kraft remarked. He reached up and rubbed his bruised, swollen chin.

The door to the Arena abruptly closed.

"Uh-oh," Boone said.

"The bastards didn't even give us any weapons!" Sergeant Havoc stated.

"We should move away from the doors," Thunder suggested.

They edged to the center of the Arena, constantly scanning the doors, waiting tensely for the Reptiloids to unleash . . . what?

Sergeant Havoc glanced at the Clansman. "I have something I want to say to you."

Kraft snickered. "Get bent!"

"I want to apologize," Havoc said.

Kraft's mouth curled downward. "Apologize? After what you did to me back there? You beat the shit out of me, you son of a bitch! We were supposed to put on a good show for the muties!"

Sergeant Havoc pursed his lips. "I know that. I was out of place. I was venting my anger over what happened to Clayboss and Rivera on you. You can't help being a jerk."

"Shove your apology up your ass!" Kraft snapped.

"Enough, already!" Boone interrupted them. "This is not the time or the place to settle your differences. Wait until we get back to California."

"If we get back," Kraft amended.

"Look!" Thunder said, pointing.

A door to their right was slowly opening. The interior was plunged in shadows, obscuring whatever was inside.

"I wish I was in Minnesota," Kraft said wistfully.

Vague forms moved from the gloom into the light.

Kraft snorted. "What is this? Some kind of a joke?"

There were four of them, all women, all skimpily attired in leather harnesses, and all of them were armed.

"These clowns must be putting us on," Kraft said.

"I don't think so," Sergeant Havoc remarked.

Three of the women were white, one black. All of them were muscular, and all of them had cropped their hair short, to just below their ears. The black woman brandished a pike. The tallest white woman, a redhead, carried a short sword and a shield. Both of the remaining two were brunettes. One of them held a green mesh net in her left hand, a dagger in her right. The last woman was armed with a five-foot trident.

"They intend to harm us," Thunder said.

"I reckon so," Boone concurred.

"Give me a break!" Kraft declared. "They're just foxes. What can they do against all of us?"

"They're armed and we're not," Sergeant Havoc observed.

"So?" Kraft rejoined. "If they try messing with us, we'll kick their butts."

The four women walked toward the Force members, their tread steady and measured, their faces grim, their weapons held in front of them at the ready.

Boone glanced at Sergeant Havoc. "Do you have a plan?"

"I was hoping you had one," Havoc responded.

"Who needs a plan?" Kraft queried sarcastically. He stepped forward several feet and placed his hands on his hips.

The women halted 15 yards off.

"What do you want?" Kraft called out.

Extending her pike toward the Clansman, the black woman spoke a few words to her companions who broke out laughing

"What's so funny?" Kraft demanded.

"You are, Pointy-Hair," the black woman replied. "You are in the Arena and you ask such a stupid question! What do you think we want?"

"You'd better not mess with us!" Kraft warned. "We've got a heavy rep!"

"I claim you for myself," the black woman told Kraft. "And before you die I will cut out your tongue."

The quartet advanced warily.

Kraft retreated until he stood next to Boone. "They're wacko!" he said.

"No," Boone stated. "They are professional fighters. I figure they have been in the Arena before. Many times before."

"Show them no mercy," Sergeant Havoc advised. "Just because they're women doesn't mean you should go easy on them. They'll kill you for sure if you do."

"I don't much like the notion of fighting a woman," Boone said. "But if it's a fight they want, then it's a fight they'll get."

With a shout of defiance, the four women charged their opponents. The black woman, true to her pledge, went after Kraft. The redhead bore down on Boone. Thunder was attacked by the brunette with the trident, while the woman with the net and dagger closed on Sergeant Havoc.

The noncom was determined to end his contest as quickly as possible so he could aid his comrades. He assumed the Kake-ashi-tachi, intending to spin-kick her into the middle of next week. But she had other ideas.

The female gladiator made an apparently reckless lunge with the gleaming dagger clutched in her left hand.

Havoc, surprised at her sloppy style, easily sidestepped to the right.

Which was exactly what the woman wanted. As the trooper was shifting his position and was momentarily off balance, she swept her mesh net around and in at ankle height. The upper third of the net wrapped tightly around the noncom's ankles, weighted by beads of metal stitched into the outer seam.

Havoc felt the constricting net enfold his ankles, and he desperately threw himself backwards, straining to extricate his legs. The net impeded his movement and refused to budge, and his momentum caused him to lose his footing. He tumbled onto his back.

With a cry of triumph, the gladiator sprang, going for a speedy kill, angling her dagger at the soldier's neck.

Havoc was ready. His ankles were tangled in the net, but he could still move his legs. He twisted and swung his legs to block her approach, his knees tucked against his chest.

The woman tried to circle to the right.

Havoc lashed out with his boots, his heels slamming into her left knee.

There was a distinct crack and the gladiator gasped and stumbled onto her right knee, her face contorted in anguish.

Havoc brought his legs up to his chest and struck again, planting both heels squarely on the point of her nose.

The gladiator's nasal cartilage crunched and she was flung onto her back, her right hand releasing the net.

Move! Havoc's mind screamed. He sat up and tugged at the mesh, swiftly unwinding the net.

Groaning, the center of her face a bloody ruins, the woman was striving to rise.

Sergeant Havoc tore the last of the mesh from his ankles and pushed himself erect. He saw his foe on her hands and knees, took one short step, and delivered a brutal kick to the right side of her head. She dropped, rolling onto her left side, exposing her neck. Without hesitation, he arced his right hand up and down, using the Tegatana, the knifehand, to finish her off. The calloused outer edge of his hand crushed her throat.

The gladiator gurgled, convulsed, wheezed, and died.

Havoc straightened and whirled, looking for someone to help.

Thunder and the brunette with the trident were ten yards away. The brunette was striving to impale the Indian on the three points of her weapon, but the Flathead was easily evading her.

Boone was also faring well.

The redhead was attempting to connect with a swipe of her short sword, and her frustration was clearly written on her features. Boone was always one step ahead of her, constantly backpedaling.

Kraft, though, was in serious trouble. The black woman seemed to be toying with him, playfully jabbing at him with her pike. Kraft darted to the right and the left, but he was never able to get out of the pike's range.

Sergeant Havoc ran toward them, a sense of guilt troubling his conscience. He shouldn't have treated Kraft so shabbily. Sure, the Clansman had no business being on the Force. And true, Kraft was a monumental pain in the butt. But Kraft wasn't totally responsible for his actions; he simply couldn't control his immature temper and his aggravating personality. Havoc wanted to make amends, somehow, if he ever got the chance.

He never did.

Kraft tripped and fell onto his right side. He surged to his knees, frantically scrambling to regain his footing.

Never missing a stride, the woman whipped the shaft of her pike around and pounded the Clansman on the temple.

Kraft was staggered by the blow. He bent backwards, sagging, unable to defend himself.

Cackling, the black gladiator raised her pike overhead.

"No!" Sergeant Havoc yelled in a desperate bid to distract her. "Try me!"

The woman's right arm descended.

Sergeant Havoc was five feet from them when he saw the sharp tip of the pike penetrate Kraft's chest squarely above the heart. The pike passed completely through the Clansman's body with deceptive ease.

Kraft screamed as he died.

The black woman glanced at Havoc as she tried to wrest the pike from her victim's torso.

Havoc felt a burning rage engulf him. He reached the gladiator in a single leap, crashing a Uraken, a left back fist, into her mouth. She released the pike and tottered backwards, bringing up her fists in a reflexive protective action. Havoc feinted with his left hand, and when she opened her guard by counterthrusting with her right, he used his right hand in a Nihon-nukite. His index and middle fingers stabbed into her eyes.

The gladiator backed away, blinking her eyes in an effort to clear her blurry vision.

His eyes blazing, Havoc leaped into the air and connected with a side jump kick. The ball of his right foot, reinforced by his combat boot heel, caught her on the point of her chin, snapping her mouth closed and her head to the rear. Her teeth splintered, blood and spittle spewing from her lips.

Whining, the woman staggered. "No! Please!" she blubbered.

Havoc paid no attention. Consumed by his fury, he rained a hail of blows on the gladiator, overpowering her feeble resistance, hitting her again and again and again. The world spun and tilted as his frenzy rose, then abruptly peaked. He suddenly realized he was on the ground, straddling the woman, his knuckles caked with crimson and pulp.

The woman was dead, her face a battered shambles, her tongue protruding from the right corner of her mouth, her eyes wide and glazing fast.

Stunned by his loss of control, Havoc stood. He turned, seeking the others.

Thunder and the brunette were less than four yards distant, the brunette continuing to try and stick him with her trident.

Boone and the redhead were likewise going at it, 20 feet to the left.

Sergeant Havoc dashed to Kraft. The Clansman was slumped on the dirt on his left side, a spreading pool of blood under him, his eyes closed, an odd grin on his face. The pike dangled from Kraft's chest, the shaft resting on the earth. Havoc leaned over and gripped the shaft, gazing for a second at the Clansman. "Sorry," he said softly, and then he yanked the pike out and straightened.

Three yards away the brunette with the trident was gaining ground on Thunder, her back to the noncom.

His lips a grim line, Havoc held the pike at chest height, extended the razor point, and sprinted toward the brunette. He aimed the tip of the pike between her shoulder blades, and in two strides he was close enough to spear the pike into her body.

Screeching, the brunette stiffened as she was impaled. The bloody point tore through her flesh between her breasts and jutted upward. She endeavored to turn, but her legs buckled and she fell forward.

Sergeant Havoc let her fall. He grabbed the trident from her lifeless left hand and pivoted.

Boone and the redhead were grappling on the turf, rolling over and over. The redhead had dropped her shield and they were wrestling for control of the sword.

Havoc raced to Boone's assistance. He reached them just as Boone succeeded in pinning the redhead. Boone's hands were clamped on the redhead's wrists, his legs aslant across her own. Havoc could see the woman's face over Boone's left shoulder. Her eyes flicked up toward him.

Thunder shouted from the noncom's rear. "Havoc! Don't!"

Havoc did. He buried the trident in the gladiator's face, the outer prongs piercing her startled eyes while the middle prong skewered her nose. She shrieked and bucked.

Boone rolled to the right and stood. He gaped at the woman, then at Havoc.

Sergeant Havoc held onto the trident until the gladiator ceased moving. He released the shaft and stepped back.

"You didn't need to do that!" Boone blurted. "I had her!"

Thunder joined them. "Havoc killed all four of them," he stated.

"What?" Boone responded, starting to turn, to scan the Arena floor.

"Kraft is dead," Thunder added solemnly.

"Kraft!" Boone spotted the Clansman and ran over. He knelt and examined the body.

Thunder stared at the noncom. "Are you all right?"

"I'm fine," Havoc answered, watching the blood flow from the last gladiator's eyes.

"What got into you?" Thunder inquired.

Havoc glanced at the Flathead. "I'm a soldier, remember? This is what I do best. It's what I do for a living. And it's about damn time we started acting like a military unit instead of a sewing circle!"

Thunder's features softened. "I regret Kraft's passing too."

"Kraft's death has nothing to do with this!" Sergeant Havoc snapped.

Boone walked toward them, downcast. "Kraft is dead," he said, as if he couldn't believe it.

"We'd better get set," Sergeant Havoc suggested. "They're bound to throw something else at us."

"Look," Thunder said, pointing at the big platform.

Reptilian was on his feet. He scrutinized the audience, which was strangely quiet. "Citizens of the Province!" his voice boomed. "It appears these games shall be more entertaining than we dared imagine! These outsiders have proven themselves valorous! They have defeated four of our favorite fighters, and in so doing have amply demonsrated their prowess! They deserve a round of applause!"

On cue, the audience erupted in applause.

Reptilian waited for the clapping to subside, then went on. "We salute you, outsiders!" he addressed the Force men.

Sergeant Havoc flipped him the finger.

Reptilian smiled. "Yes! These games promise to be the most exciting we have ever held! All thanks to you! But you must be fatigued after your bout. You will be permitted to eat and rest, to refresh yourselves for your next contest!"

Sergeant Havoc pointed at Kraft. "What about him, you bastard? We want his body buried!"

Reptilian smirked. "I'm sorry. Burial is not possible." He paused. "We never waste meat."

The door under the royal platform swung out, disgorging ten Reptiloids with pikes. Five formed a line to the left, five to the right.

"Again, we salute you!" Reptilian declared. He motioned toward the door.

"I say we stay here and fight!" Sergeant Havoc stated angrily.

"And commit suicide?" Boone remarked. "No way. We can all use a rest. We need time to plan."

"I agree with Boone," Thunder said.

Sergeant Havoc glanced at Kraft's corpse and bowed his head. "Okay. For now. But I won't take much more of this!"

They strolled wearily in the direction of the door.

Sergeant Havoc gazed up at Blade. The Warrior was in a chair, glaring balefully at Reptilian, surrounded by Reptiloids. "Some head of the Force he is! He just sits there while one of his men dies!"

Boone looked up at Blade. "He doesn't have any choice. Look at all those mutants."

"I see them," Havoc said. "But if I'd been up there, I would have done something. I don't know what, but something." He frowned. "You know, I used to admire Blade a lot. Now I'm not so sure."

"Don't be so hard on him," Boone commented, his tone laced with annoyance. "He did the right thing. What good would it have done him to be killed needlessly?"

"Well, while Blade sits up there doing nothing," Havoc said, "there's one thing you'd better keep in mind."

"What's that?" Boone asked.

"One of us has already died," Boone snapped bitterly. "Which one of us will be next?"

CHAPTER FIFTEEN

Not another one!

Dear Spirit, no!

Not another one!

Blade watched a detail of human slaves remove the bodies from the Arena. He noticed their rough manner as they handled Kraft, and his veins stood out on his temples. For the first time in his life he thirsted for vengeance with a powerful passion. Emotion ruled his temperament instead of his typical logic. He wanted to make the Reptiloids pay for their bloodthirsty tyranny! He wanted to see them suffer! Most of all, he wanted to get his hands around Reptilian's neck!

"Aren't you enjoying our games?" Reptilian asked. He was reclining in his chair, his features reflecting an attitude of smug satisfaction.

Blade's gray eyes bored into the mutant's. "I'm going to kill you."

Reptilian chuckled. "Really? Somehow I doubt it. If you make any hostile moves, my personal guards will slay you on the spot."

"I don't know when," Blade reiterated. "But I'm going to kill you. You don't deserve to live."

"Who are you to judge me?" Reptilian responded acidly. "Humans are hardly qualified to sit in judgment on mutants!"

"No matter which species is involved," Blade said, "murderous psychopaths are all the same. They all deserve a similar fate. Summary execution."

"You are judging me by human standards," Reptilian stated. "By mutant standards I am a paragon of virtue."

"Then mutants must have pitiful standards," Blade commented.

Reptilian studied the giant for a minute. "You are understandably upset about the death of one of your men. Perhaps you should not be here when they return."

"How long will that be?" Blade inquired.

"Several hours," Reptilian revealed. "There are other contests we must observe first."

"Which one will I be in?" Blade asked.

"You?"

"Surely you're not going to keep me on this platform during all the contests?" Blade queried.

"That's exactly what I am going to do," Reptilian said. "Except for when your men return. I may have you returned to your cell."

"I'm really not going to be in any of your so-called games?" Blade demanded.

Reptilian shook his head. "You may view them, but you will not participate."

"Why?"

"I will explain everything later," Reptilian said.

"I want to know now," Blade persisted.

Reptilian sighed. "Very well. We have a few minutes to spare before the next bout." He gazed out over the Arena. "Earlier we were discussing the different dietary requirements of humans and Reptiloids. I mentioned a certain system I've developed when it comes to the consuming of humans."

"I remember," Blade commented.

"As I mentioned, human meat is a delicacy for us," Reptilian said. "We primarily reserve the consumption of humans for special occasions. By intentionally limiting the number of humans we consume, we reduce the inevitable adverse reaction in our human slave population. They know if they cooperate with us, they may never be eaten. If they work hard and obey us diligently, they can live to old age. Once they do, they're safe, because we are not fond of consuming the flesh of the elderly. It's too stringy, and nowhere near as tasty." He paused. "To further reduce the prospects of a rebellion, I have established a system of selective consumption. We will eat outsiders before we touch a member of our core slave population. This explains why we send out so many Hunter Squads. We don't want to run out of outsiders. Unless our slaves violate one of our rules and regulations, they are relatively safe. This condition gives them a glimmer of hope on which to base their lives, and it reduces the risk of a rebellion."

"You have everything figured out, don't you?" Blade commented.

"I am Reptilian," the mutant said. "I can do no less."

"So what about me?" Blade inquired. "Why aren't you going

to throw me in the Arena?"

"Because I don't want you damaged," Reptilian said.

"Why not?"

Reptilian stared at the Warrior. "Because I am quite fussy about my food."

"Food!" Blade blurted.

"Of course," Reptilian said. "Did you think we would become bosom buddies?" He snickered. "I will not eat just any human. I prefer one with outstanding physical and mental attributes. You qualify as such a one."

"Lucky me!" Blade quipped.

"When I was informed about your fight with the Hunter Squad, I knew you were right for me," Reptilian said. "Very few humans can hold their own against us in the forest. But you did. You even killed several of my subjects. Only a human endowed with great strength and ability could have accomplished such a feat. You are just the sort of meat I like the most."

"If you intend to eat me," Blade said, "why are you being so nice now?"

"I enjoy getting to know the human I consume beforehand," Reptilian explained. "My meal is that much more delectable. Perhaps an analogy will suffice. I know humans in other parts of the country raise animals for food. Cows, chickens, turkeys, and the like. Imagine you had spent years raising a cow or steer to feed your family. When the time came to butcher the animal, you might be somewhat sad because you had grown attached to it. But at the same time, the meat from that steer or cow would be some of the best-tasting meat you'd ever eaten. Do you follow me?"

Blade simply glowered.

"So now you know," Reptilian said.

"You'll never succeed," Blade declared. "You know that, don't you?"

"At what? Consuming you?" Reptilian grinned.

"No. At establishing your Mutant Era, as you call it," Blade said. "We will stop you."

"Humans stop us?" Reptilian responded, and laughed. "Your pathetic species is on the eclipse and doesn't have the brains to recognize its own demise!"

"Don't count the human species out yet," Blade cautioned. "We will rebuild the world. We will produce a civilization better than the one which nearly destroyed the planet."

"It's a little late for that, don't you think?" Reptilian rejoined. "Your species had its chance and you blew it. Mutantkind will do better. We will fashion a Utopia."

Blade snorted derisively. "Is the Province your idea of a Utopia?"

"Utopian civilizations take time to construct," Reptilian replied. "They are not produced overnight. Rome, as the saying goes, was not built in a day."

Blade glanced at the small platform to his right. "Do the other leaders in the New Order agree with you?"

Reptilian gazed at the seven diverse mutants and frowned. "we do not see eye to eye on everything. But they will come around to my way of thinking eventually. If we can turn Grizzly around, we can turn any mutant."

Blade straightened, astounded. "Grizzly? He's here?"

Reptilian smirked. "How thoughtless of me. Did I forget to mention we had captured him and the lovely Ms. Morris?"

"Athena too!" Blade exclaimed.

Reptilian relished the Warrior's stunned countenance. "Did you honestly think they would elude us? I have given orders they are not to be harmed, not until Grizzly has demonstrated where his loyalties lie. Gat has held several profitable conversations with him, and Gat is of the opinion Grizzly will come over to our side. Grizzly, as you no doubt are aware, is not very fond of humans."

Grizzly turning traitor? The idea dazed Blade. He knew Grizzly disliked the human race, but would the bear-man actually betray the Force?

"So what is it going to be?" Reptilian inquired. "Do you want to remain here when your men return for their next contest, or would you rather go back to your cell?"

Blade slumped in his chair. "I'd like to return to my cell now, if you don't mind."

"Now? And miss all the fun?" Reptilian responded scornfully. "Very well. I find your attitude depressing. You may return to your cell." He glanced at one of his personal guards. "Tur, take this morbid excuse for a sentient being back to his cell. Take ten others with you to insure he doesn't attempt to escape. Leave four to watch the cell, then return. I wouldn't want you to miss the games."

"As you will, my liege," Tur said. He prodded Blade with his pike. "Let's go, human! On your feet!"

Blade slowly rose, the picture of depression.

Reptilian snickered. "Do you see him, Captain Tur? This is the man who claims humans will defeat us?"

Captain Tur laughed.

"I just hope when it comes times to eat him," Reptilian commented, "he doesn't give me indigestion! I hear Clayboss and Rivera were on the lean, stringy side." He cackled in sadistic glee.

PART FIVE
OF MEN AND MUTANTS

CHAPTER SIXTEEN

"Where have all the guards gone?" Athena asked.

Grizzly, seated on the cot, looked up. "What do you mean?"

"There aren't as many as there were before," Athena said. She was standing next to the door, gazing out the barred window. "There were six out there at one time. Now there are only two. I wonder where the rest went." She paused. "And there hasn't been as much traffic in the corridor."

"The Arena games must have begun," Grizzly mentioned.

"Those horrid contests Gat was telling us about?" Athena asked.

Grizzly nodded. He rose and moved to her side. "This could be the chance I've been waiting for."

"But how will we break out of here?" Athena questioned.

"We may not have to," Grizzly said.

"What?"

Grizzly nodded at the small window. "Here comes our gift horse."

Puzzled, Athena looked out the window.

The Prefect was approaching their cell, a pike in his right hand. He motioned for the guards to unlock the door.

Grizzly stepped back from the door and and drew Athena with him.

"Greetings," Gat said as he entered, all smiles. "Reptilian asked me to stop by."

"When do we get to meet Reptilian?" Grizzly inquired. "I was hoping we would before this."

"Reptilian has been busy with the preparations for the games," Gat replied. "He sends his regards."

"When will we be allowed out of our cell?" Grizzly queried.

"Not for a while, I'm afraid," Gat said. "Reptilian is still not convinced you can be trusted."

"What can I do to convince him?"

"Reptilian has a test in mind for you," Gat stated. "You must prove yourself to his satisfaction. He was most disappointed when you refused to eat your burgers."

"I don't much like humans," Grizzly said, "but I've never eaten one before."

"Try them. You'll like them," Gat assured him.

A biting retort was on the tip of Athena's tongue, but she held her peace. Grizzly had explained to her the necessity of not antagonizing the Reptiloids, not if they wanted to acquire their trust.

"What is this about a test?" Grizzly asked.

Gat smiled. "You will see. Very shortly."

"Any word on the other Force members?" Grizzly inquired politely.

"Why should you care?" Gat responded. "They are your enemies. You must never forget that."

Grizzly surreptitiously glanced at the cell door. Both of the guards were leaning against the far wall, pikes in hand, conversing. Gat was standing slightly to the right of the doorway.

"Reptilian is a patient mutant," Gat was saying, "but his patience has limits. Don't take forever making up your mind."

"Tell me," Grizzly urged. "Why is it so important for me to wholeheartedly embrace your cause? Why is Reptilian going to so much trouble to convert me?"

"Because of the propaganda value," Gat divulged. "You've lived among the humans. You've accepted their way of life. But if we can turn you around, if we can make you see the light, your conversion will help to convince other mutants living with our hated enemy. We know there are other mutants living in the Civilized Zone and elsewhere. Even a few of the leaders of the New Order harbor secret sympathies for the humans. We want you to tell them the truth. Tell them about the miserable treatment mutants receive at the hands of the bigoted humans. Tell them about the prejudice you have faced. Tell them the humans are a vile, wicked race, who deserve to be subjugated. Humans are only good for one thing; to function as slaves."

Athena couldn't keep quiet any longer. "Slaves? Why can't humans and mutants live as friends?"

"It will never happen," Gat asserted. "Think back on your human history. Human beings have never been able to live in peace with their own kind, let alone another species. The white race came close to destroying the red race and enslaved the black. The blacks despised the whites. The yellow race distrusted everyone." He laughed. "If humanity could not live at peace with itself, how in the hell do you expect your species to live in peace with us?"

"We've learned from our mistakes," Athena said. "As a race, we've finally learned the value of peace."

Gat shook his head, smirking. "We must not live on the same planet. Where on this world is your race at peace? The Russians control a section of what was once the eastern United States, and they are locked in a life-or-death struggle with your Freedom Federation."

"You know about the Freedom Federation?" Athena inquired in surprise.

Grizzly took a casual step toward the doorway.

"Of course," Gat answered her. "We have contacts in the black market and elsewhere who keep us informed. And the major we captured, Enright, told us a lot before he died."

Athena knew about Enright; General Gallagher had provided details of the major's doomed reconnaissance run prior to their meeting with Blade. "Enright is dead?"

"Yes," Gat verified, smacking his lips. "And he was quite tasty, I must admit."

Grizzly took another step in the direction of the doorway. He was now three feet from Gat, five from the door.

Athena bowed her head. "This is like a living nightmare," she muttered.

"Did I upset you?" Gat asked facetiously. "My! What a pity!"

Grizzly draped his hands at his sides.

"Well, I must be off," Gat said. "I don't want to miss too many of the contests."

"Will we get to see any of these contests?" Grizzly asked.

"Yes, you will," Gat replied, grinning wickedly. "Very soon, in fact."

"Before you go," Grizzly stated, "there's something I'd like to say to you."

"What is it?" Gat inquired hopefully. "Have you come to your senses at last? Are you ready to pledge your loyalty to the mutant cause?"

"What I have to say is this," Grizzly said, taking one more

stride, speaking softly. His features abruptly hardened. "You are, without a doubt, one of the most suck-egg sons of bitches I've ever met. If you expect me to turn against the Force, forget it, chump! When I joined up, I gave my word to serve for one year, to take on any threats to the Freedom Federation. My word may not mean much to you, shit-for-brains, but it means everything to me. If you don't keep your word, whether you're a mutant or a human, then you're not worth beans as a person. Of course, I wouldn't expect a scumbag like you to understand that."

Gat's lips were moving but he couldn't seem to find his voice. "You dare!" he finally bellowed.

The two guards in the corridor ceased their discussion and straightened.

"I will inform Reptilian of your allegiance to the humans," Gat told Grizzly. "I will recommend immediate execution."

Alerted by Gat's tone of voice, the pair of guards came toward the cell to see what was happening.

Grizzly raised his hands to waist high. "I don't think so."

"What?" Gat said.

"I don't think you're going to live long enough to tell Reptilian anything," Grizzly stated grimly, his hands rising to his chest.

Gat was clearly perplexed by Grizzly's confidence. "Don't try anything!" he warned. "The odds are three to one."

Grizzly grinned. "Which means I have the edge."

The two guards walked over to the cell door.

Gat glanced at them, and reassured by their presence he made bold to taunt Grizzly. "I knew it! I knew you couldn't be trusted!"

"I didn't fool you for a minute, did I?" Grizzly asked sarcastically.

"Not for a minute!" Gat replied belligerently.

"Sure I didn't," Grizzly said contemptuously, then sighed. "Well, I guess we've said all that needs to be said. Suppose we get right down to cases."

Gat gripped his pike with both hands. "Don't even think it!"

Ignoring the Prefect, Grizzly looked at Athena. "When I cut loose, don't move. Stay right where you are."

Gat snickered. "Cut loose? What the hell do you mean, cut loose?"

Grizzly beamed and held his hands out, palms inward. "Just

this." He slowly uncurled his fingers until his digits were fully extended, and as he tensed his hand muscles, as he locked his fingers in place, his claws snapped out, sliding from the hidden sheaths in his fingers and protruding from under the flaps behind his fingernails.

"What the . . . !" Gat exclaimed at the sight of the five-inch claws and lowering the tip of his pike.

Grizzly suddenly crouched and growled, his hands dropping to his sides. He took a menacing step toward the Prefect.

Gat reacted by taking a stride backward, inadvertently putting himself in the doorway between Grizzly and the guards.

"I noticed someone did a number on you," Grizzly said in a guttural tone. "I'm going to finish the job!"

Gat hissed and jabbed his pike at his foe.

Transfixed by the tableau, Athena watched with baited breath as Grizzly went into action. She saw him easily sidestep the pike thrust and close on Gat. Grizzly speared his right hand up and in, and those deadly claws of his ripped into Gat's throat below the chin, angled upwards.

Gat's red eyes widened in stark stupefaction.

Grizzly, his claws buried to the fingernails in the Prefect's throat, added insult to injury. "Just as I thought!" he declared scornfully. "You're a wimp!"

Gat dropped the pike and grasped at Grizzly's right hand, but he was unable to sustain his grip. Green blood was pouring from his ravaged neck, a virtual torrent. He gasped and gawked at Grizzly, his eyelids fluttering.

The guards were trying to enter the cell, but they were stymied because Grizzly was holding the Prefect's body as a shield in the doorway. They couldn't see Grizzly's claws in Gat's neck; they mistakenly believed Grizzly had hold of the Prefect's neck. Their misimpression was rudely shattered when the guard on the right glanced down and observed the Prefect's blood spilling onto the floor. "Prefect!" he shouted, and tried to shove past Gat's body.

Grizzly yanked his claws free and shoved, sending the Prefect staggering backwards into the guards. One of the guards caught the Prefect under the shoulders and eased Gat to the corridor floor while the second attacked.

Athena, as always, was dazzled by Grizzly's speed. He dodged the second guard's pike and brought his left hand up, his arm a streak as he imbedded his claws in the guard's eyes, then raked them to the right.

With a terrified screech, the Reptiloid released his pike and placed his hands over the ragged furrow where his eyes had been a moment before. He uttered a sobbing sound and stumbled to the left.

Grizzly finished the hapless Reptiloid off with two quick swipes across the guard's neck. Gurgling and gushing blood, the Reptiloid collapsed.

"Look out!" Athena cried as the other guard charged through the doorway.

Grizzly, watching the dying Reptiloid sprawl onto its abdomen, almost lost his life. The other guard's pike grazed his chest as he twisted aside, drawing a thin line of blood. Unable to check his pell-mell lunge, the Reptiloid swung his shaft at Grizzly's head. Grizzly ducked under the blow and rammed both arms forward, imbedding both sets of claws in the guard's stomach. With his massive shoulder muscles heaving, he swept his arms upward, opening the Reptiloid from the navel to the sternum.

Athena grimaced as the Reptiloid's internal organs oozed from the cavity.

"No!" the guard wailed, his horrified gaze riveted to his stomach. "No!"

"Yes, sucker!" Grizzly snapped.

The Reptiloid clutched at his organs in a vain attempt to tuck them inside his body. But the slimy jumble of tubelike intestines and other organs slipped through his fingers. He tottered and tossed his pike aside. "No!" he said weakly.

Grizzly glanced at Athena. "This is it! Let's go!" He ran from the cell.

Athena took a last look at the gutted Reptiloid as the creature sagged to the floor, then she took off after her companion.

Grizzly was ten feet away to the right. "Come on!" he goaded her. "Don't be a slowpoke!"

Athena's left foot bumped something and she gazed downward. Gat was on his back, his hands on his chest, his eyes open but empty.

"Come on!" Grizzly prompted.

Athena nodded and jogged after him as he led her down the

corridor to a door which she opened. "It's a stairwell! Which way?"

"Gat told us the Arena is on the lowest level," Grizzly reminded her. "That's where we should find the others." He started down.

Athena followed. They descended two levels when Grizzly abruptly halted.

"Sssshhh!" he cautioned her.

Athena listened but could hear nothing.

"Someone is coming up these stairs," Grizzly informed her. "Come on." He nodded at the door and waited impatiently as she opened it. "Quickly!"

They sprinted along the hallway for dozens of yards.

Athena happened to glance to her right, and the word she read on a sign on a closed door brought her up short. "Grizzly!"

Grizzly stopped and turned. "What?"

"Look!" Athena exclaimed.

Grizzly stared at the door, reading the sign. ARMORY. He grinned and stepped to her side. "Just what the doctor ordered."

Athena looked in both directions. "Why aren't there any guards?"

Grizzly shrugged. "Who knows? Maybe they're all down in the Arena watching the games. Maybe they don't post guards here. Maybe they've become complacent because the humans have never revolted. Who gives a damn? He grabbed at the doorknob, forgetting his claws were fully extended. When his fingers were rigid and his claws out, he was unable to use his hands for any other purpose than ripping and slashing. He could not bend his hand or employ his fingers for gripping objects. Only after he relaxed his digits, after his claws were automatically retracted, could he use his fingers to hold anything. "Damn!" he muttered as his claws raked the door.

"Allow me," Athena offered, seizing the knob and trying to turn it. "It's locked!" she informed him.

"Stand back," Grizzly directed. He took a pace backwards, then brought his right leg up, delivering a shattering kick alongside the doorknob.

The door shook but held fast. It was obviously reinforced.

"Someone will hear!" Athena stated apprehensively.

"Let them!" Grizzly declared. He kicked the door a second time and was thwarted again.

"You're making too much noise!" Athena protested.

"You need a weapon," Grizzly told her. "Unless you plan to use spitballs against the Reptiloids." He kicked the door a third time.

A fracture appeared next to the knob, six inches in length and a quarter of an inch wide.

"We're almost there!" Grizzly gloated.

"What's that?" Athena queried anxiously, glancing at the door at the other end of the hall, believing she had heard an indistinct sound.

She had.

Reptiloids were surging through the door at the end of the hall, all of them armed with pikes. Six. Eight. Ten. Fourteen. She lost count. "Grizzly!" she cried, distraught.

Grizzly kicked the door a final time. The fracture widened and lengthened but the door did not open.

"Grizzly!" Athena shouted, backing against the wall.

Enraged beyond his endurance, Grizzly faced the charging Reptiloids, raised his arms above his head, and roared his defiant challenge.

CHAPTER SEVENTEEN

Blade walked with his head bowed, his eyes downcast, behind the captain of the escort to his cell.

Captain Tur looked over his left shoulder at the prisoner and snickered. "Look at this wretch!" he stated for the benefit of his ten companions following Blade. "A superb example of Homo sapiens!"

Several of the Reptiloids laughed.

"Yes, sir," commented one of them. "They are saps. That's for sure."

More laughter.

They were walking up a stairwell, their captive a study in misery. Not one of them entertained the slightest notion their prisoner would cause them any trouble. He was too depressed, perhaps on the verge of an emotional collapse. Or so they reasoned.

But they were wrong.

Blade prepared himself. He estimated they were about four levels below the ground floor, below the cell block. The stairwell bothered him; although he wasn't positive, he doubted it was the same stairwell he had used before. The placement of the lanterns seemed to be different. How many stairwells were there in the Imperium? he speculated. Probably a large number. The Imperium was huge, a maze of corridors and rooms. But he should be able to find his way down to the Arena without any difficulty after rescuing the others. He . . .

Wait a minute!

Blade almost gave himself away, almost snapped his head up in consternation, but he suppressed the impulse. Maybe he was making a mistake! He planned to scour the cells above, find the Force members, then descend to the Arena and kill Reptilian at all costs. Reptilian was, as General Gallagher had said, the brains behind the operation. If Reptilian died, the New Order might very well come unglued. Without a forceful leader, any organization ultimately decayed and disintegrated.

But what if he was wrong?

What if Boone, Thunder, and Havoc were not in one of the cells? What if they were being held somewhere in the Arena, awaiting their next contest? Would the Reptiloids go to all the bother to take them all the way up to the cells between bouts? The prospect was not very likely. Still, searching the cells would not be a complete waste of time. Grizzly and Athena must be in one of them.

He hoped.

Captain Tur unexpectedly turned and prodded the giant with his pike. "Move your ass, human! We want to see the games!"

Blade gazed down at the point of the pike pressing against his stomach and exploded. He gripped the shaft below the point and wrenched, jerking the pike from Captain Tur's hands. With a savage swipe he rammed the butt end of the shaft into Tur's throat, then twirled the pike, swinging the tip outward, and spun.

The Reptiloids on the stairs below took a second to galvanize themselves. The first one mindlessly lunged at the Warrior and received the business end of the pike in his right eye for his effort. He screamed as the point penetrated his brain, and then he was flung backwards, his consciousness fading as his body collided with those below.

Three of the Reptiloids went down in a chain reaction, sprawling onto the stairs. The rest charged.

Blade met them with a grin creasing his features. His gray eyes sparkled as he avoided a pike and stabbed his own into the neck of a mutant. He wrested the tip free in time to block another blow, and retaliated with a sweep of his pike into the groin of one of his opponents.

The Reptiloid doubled over, screeching, and was knocked down the stairs by those striving to reach the Warrior.

Blade found the pike to be an exceptional weapon. Its length enabled him to keep the Reptiloids at bay; they didn't dare get too close for fear of being lanced. Conversely, his pike handily deflected their jabs. For a minute the conflict was in doubt, but he adroitly held his own.

One of the Reptiloids tried to stab the giant's right kneecap.

Blade dodged to the left to protect his knee and in so doing accidentally saved his life.

There was the pad of rushing feet, and Captain Tur hurtled past the Warrior, narrowly missing him, flying through the space he had occupied but a fraction of a second before. Tur plummeted into his fellow mutants, bowling five of them over. Two of them lost their footing and sailed over the railing, shrieking as they fell.

Suddenly Blade had the upper hand.

Only one of the guards had retained his footing. The rest were struggling to disentangle themselves and scramble erect.

With a prodigious bound Blade was among them. He smashed the shaft of his pike into the Reptiloid still standing and sent the mutant tumbling down the stairs. Two more of the Reptiloids were speared in the face before they could get to their feet. Another mutant did rise, and promptly received the pike tip in his jugular.

Captain Tur was on his hands and knees, shaking his head, dazed.

The last Reptiloid stood with his pike in his right hand.

Blade took a stride and kicked Tur in the mouth. The captain collapsed. Blade was about to plant his pike in Tur's neck when he detected a motion out of the corner of his eyes and whirled.

Just as the last guard hurled his pike.

Blade tried to throw himself to the right to avoid the gleaming point, but he wasn't entirely successful. He felt the pike bite into his left shoulder and an intense pain shot through him. The tip gouged an inch-deep groove in his flesh, scraping the bone and tearing his black leather vest, but the force of the Reptiloid's toss propelled the pike ten feet past him. Blade instantly retaliated by flinging his pike, with better results.

The Reptiloid was scanning the stairs for another pike he could use when the Warrior's weapon caught him in the chest. He was flung backwards by the impact and clattered and thudded down the stairs.

Blade sagged against the railing, his shoulder throbbing, blood flowing from the wound, abruptly dizzy. He surveyed the stairwell, expecting another attack, but none of the Reptiloids were moving.

He'd done it!

Blade inspected his injury, frowning at the sight of the jagged tissue. The blood flow was not very great, indicating the pike had missed a vital vein or artery. He couldn't afford to expend precious time doctoring the wound now. It would have to wait.

First things first.

Blade walked to a fallen pike and retrieved the weapon.
Grimacing in discomfort, he headed up the stairs toward the
ground level. He would need to search each and every cell to find
Grizzly and Athena. If only he knew where the armory Prine had
told him about was located! With his left shoulder injured, his
effectiveness in combat would be diminished. He flexed the fingers
of his left hand, pleased his dexterity was not impaired.

But could he use a pike with the injured arm?

Blade halted and took hold of the shaft with both hands. He
tried a few tentative swings. His left shoulder twinged with pangs
of agony, but he could use his arm if necessary. Satisfied, he
gripped the pike in his right hand and resumed his ascent.

What was that?

He was on the third-level landing when he heard the harsh
clamor coming from the corridor beyond the landing door.

Voices were shouting.

There were screams and cries of torment.

What was going on?

Blade cautiously stepped to the door and gingerly opened it a
crack.

A savage fracas greeted his wondering gaze.

A battle royal was being waged at the far end of the corridor
between Grizzly and a detail of Reptiloids. Seven or eight of the
lizard-men were down, and the rest were trying to impale Grizzly
on their pikes. The confines of the corridor prevented them from
rushing him all at once, so they came at him two or three at a
time. Grizzly's claws parried thrust after thrust, and if a Reptiloid
miscalculated and came a little too close, he ripped him open.

Athena stood against the hall wall midway between the
stairwell Blade was in and the fight raging at the opposite end.

Blade threw the door open and raced toward them. Grizzly's
back was to him, but several of the Reptiloids saw him
approaching and renewed their efforts to slay Grizzly.

Athena, engrossed in watching the brutal brawl, did not realize
anyone else was in the corridor until a heavy hand fell on her right
shoulder. She involuntarily jumped and turned, relief washing
over her features. "Blade!"

"Stay here!" Blade directed, and started to go to Grizzly's aid.

"Wait!" Athena cried, clutching his arm. "Look!" she said, pointing at the ARMORY door.

Blade paused. The armory! He glanced at Grizzly, noting the mutant was holding his own, at least for the moment. But the Reptiloids threatened to overwhelm him at any second.

"We've got to help him!" Athena urged.

Blade gazed at the armory door, noticing the cracks.

"Grizzly tried to kick it in!" Athena told him.

Blade leaned the pike against the wall and reached for the knob, intending to batter the door down, but his fingertips merely brushed the doorknob and the door unexpectedly swung inward. Blade hurried inside.

Athena followed, glancing at the lock. The inner side of the jamb in which the lock was imbedded was hanging in strips. Grizzly's last kick must have shattered it! She looked up, almost bumping into Blade.

The Warrior had stopped a few feet in the chamber. The armory was plunged in darkness, the light from the hallway revealing a few crates and the vague outline of gun racks.

Athena recalled seeing several lanterns in the corridor. "I'll be right back!" she declared, and ran out.

Blade moved toward the gun racks, his keen eyes probing the gloom. He needed something with firepower, and he needed it quickly. His left knee bumped against the edge of a wooden crate.

Damn!

Bright light illuminated the chamber as Athena suddenly returned, bearing one of the hall lanterns in her right hand.

Blade spied a table to his right, his eyes narrowing as he recognized the items piled on top of it. All of the guns and backpacks confiscated by the Reptiloids were spread out upon the table!

"Hurry!" Athena goaded him.

Blade reached the table in two strides. He scooped up the M60, found an ammo belt, and fed the ammunition into the machine gun.

Athena dashed over. "Can I help?"

Blade grabbed an M-16 and tossed the weapon to her.

Athena caught the M-16 with her left hand, deposited the lantern on the table, and swiftly checked the magazine. "Loaded," she said.

"On me," Blade stated, running from the armory, Athena on his heels.

Grizzly was in trouble. A Reptiloid with a nasty gash on its neck had its arms wrapped around his ankles and was holding on for dear life. Encumbered by the lizard-man clinging to his legs, Grizzly was on the verge of going down. He was twisted sideways, blood seeping from a half-dozen lacerations, his claws countering pike after pike.

One of the Reptiloids prepared to let fly with a pike.

"Grizzly!" Blade bellowed. "Down!"

Grizzly cast a fleeting glance in the direction of the Warrior and flattened, diving away from the Reptiloids, still ensnared by the lizard-man with the injured neck.

Blade cut loose with the big M60, the machine gun thundering, the gun bucking against his side.

Athena joined in with the M-16.

Caught with nowhere to take cover, the Reptiloids were decimated. The M60's heavy slugs tore through their bodies, stitching them with holes, blowing out large chunks of flesh from their backs. Torso after torso erupted in a geyser of green fluid and blasted tissue. The rounds from the M-16 added to the carnage. Many of the lizard-men shrieked in torment or anger as they were perforated. A few tried to flee, to retreat to the far stairwell, but they were mowed down before they could manage two strides.

Blade kept firing until the floor was littered with the dead and dying. He eased up on the trigger, his ears ringing.

Athena ceased shooting. "That felt good," she commented.

Blade walked toward Grizzly. "Are you okay?"

Grizzly tried to rise, a look of astonishment flitting across his face as he realized he was still being held about the ankles. He looked down at the Reptiloid holding his legs.

The lizard-man was wheezing, green blood spraying from its neck.

Grizzly brought both arms around and down, burying his claws in the Reptiloid's head, one hand near each ear.

With a protracted gasp the lizard-man went limp, his arms dropping to the floor.

Grizzly jumped to his feet, a sneer on his lips. "Serves you right, sucker! Nobody manhandles me."

Blade reached Grizzly's side. "Are you okay?" he reiterated.

Grizzly glanced up, grinning. "Never been better."

Athena hurried over. "You're hurt!" she exclaimed, staring at the crimson coating his chest.

"A few pricks, is all," Grizzly said. "It's nothing."

"You should be bandaged!" Athena persisted.

"There's no time for that," Blade declared brusquely. "We must find Boone, Havoc, and Thunder." He scrutinized the heap of Reptiloid forms. "We're going to pay these bastards back for everything they've done!"

Grizzly beamed. "Now you're talking!"

"What about Kraft, Clayboss, and Rivera?" Athena asked. "You didn't mention them."

Blade gazed at her and sadly shook his head.

Athena's mouth went slack. "Kraft too?"

"I saw him killed," Blade detailed. "In the Arena."

Grizzly held his gore-encrusted claws aloft. "I can't wait to meet up with more Reptiloids!"

"Back to the armory," Blade ordered, wheeling and going back in.

Grizzly knelt and wiped his claws clean on the pants leg of one of the deceased lizard-men. He slowly relaxed his fingers and his claws slid from view.

"I'm sorry," Athena apologized as Grizzly stood.

"For what?"

"I wasn't much help to you," Athena said. "I stood there and watched instead of trying to get into the armory. The door was busted and I didn't even know it."

"It's no big deal," Grizzly said.

Athena frowned. "I'm not doing very well on this mission. I thought I would be able to face anything after my Ranger training. I guess I was wrong."

"Hey!" Blade shouted, standing next to the armory door. "What are you waiting for? World War Four? Get over here right now!" He stepped back into the armory.

"What's gotten into him?" Athena queried as she hastened to comply.

"I don't know," Grizzly admitted. "But I like the change. He's pissed off about something. I have a feeling we're going to see a side of Blade we've never seen before."

"How do you mean?" Athena inquired.

"Wait and see," Grizzly replied.

Blade was sorting through the gear on the table. He discovered his Bowies in their sheaths and snatched them up. Moving rapidly, he unfastened his belt, aligned a Bowie over each hip, secured his belt, then drew the knives. They glittered in the lantern light. "If I'd had these earlier," he declared, "Kraft might still be alive."

"How do we play this?" Grizzly asked.

Blade faced them, sheathing his Bowies. "We're going to finish the job we were sent to do." He scanned the armory, noting crate after crate of explosives. "We're going to destroy this hellhole and put an end to Reptilian's insane ambition."

"Do you have a plan?" Athena questioned hopefully.

Blade nodded. "I have a plan." He looked from one to the other. "But I want one thing understood."

"What?" Athena responded.

Blade's features changed, becoming uncharacteristically, shockingly sinister. "Reptilian is mine!" he stated in a gravelly tone.

Athena did a double take. She had never seen this aspect of the giant's nature before.

Grizzly chuckled. "Now you're talking! Let's party!"

CHAPTER EIGHTEEN

"How much longer, do you think?" Boone asked.

"How should I know?" Sergeant Havoc snapped. "Your guess is as good as mine."

"He was only asking," Thunder interceded on Boone's behalf. "Why are you so angry at him?"

They were in a holding room located under the stands, not more than 20 yards from the Arena floor. Periodically they heard the roar of the crowd, the clapping and the cheering. Three trays of untouched food rested on a wooden bench situated to the right of the barred wall fronting the corridor to the Arena.

Sergeant Havoc sighed, gazing at Boone. "I'm sorry. I can't seem to control my temper. All I can think of is Kraft. I keep seeing that pike going through his chest!"

Boone and Thunder exchanged glances. They were standing near the bars. Havoc was leaning against the wall eight feet away, next to the bench.

"You can't blame yourself for what happened," Boone said.

Havoc's self-torture was transparent. He slowly shook his head. "Who else can I blame? I was the one who kicked the stuffing out of him. My beating hurt him, slowed him down enough for the gladiator to kill him."

"You don't know that," Boone disagreed. "Kraft was out of it ever since he ate those burgers. Like always, his big mouth got him into trouble. And remember, Kraft didn't possess your skill at hand-to-hand combat. Without his switchblade he wasn't much of a fighter." Boone paused, reflecting for a moment. "For that matter, without my Hombres I'm not all that great either."

Sergeant Havoc frowned. "I'll never forgive myself for what I did."

Thunder stared at the noncom. "If Kraft's time on this world was over, there was nothing you could have done to prevent his dying. We all have our alloted spans. When the Spirit calls you home, you must go."

"I'm not a fatalist," Havoc mentioned. "I believe we make our own destiny."

"To a limited degree, perhaps," Thunder said. "But my people know all life is ruled by the Spirit-In-All-Things. The Spirit rules in the affairs of men, guiding us, teaching us. And when our time is up, we head for the higher realms. The Spirit always prevails."

"So whose side is the Spirit on?" Havoc queried angrily. "Ours or Reptilians?"

Before Thunder could reply, a Reptiloid appeared on the other side of the bars. "You have five minutes," he announced, and departed.

Sergeant Havoc straightened and walked to the bars. "Good. I'm tired of waiting."

"What will they pit us against this time?" Boone wondered.

"I don't care what it is," Havoc said. "Just so I get a crack at Reptilian."

"Reptilian?" Boone scrutinized the noncom. "How do you plan to do it? Reptilian will be up on that platform. What is it? Ten feet high?"

"I'll find a way," Sergeant Havoc vowed.

"Just find a way to stay alive," Boone advised.

"Blade will find a way to help us," Thunder predicted.

Sergeant Havoc laughed, a short, bitter sound. "Blade? He'll sit on his butt and watch us die, just like he did with Kraft."

"Let's not start that again," Boone said.

They lapsed into an awkward silence, awaiting the lizard-men. Several minutes elapsed.

Boone broke the quiet. "We don't have much time, so there's something I'd like to say." He gazed at Thunder, then Havoc. "I know some of us haven't always seen eye to eye—"

"There's an understatement!" Havoc mumbled.

"But I've enjoyed being on the Force," Boone went on. "These past three months I've come to know each of you fairly well. In the Cavalry we place a high value on honor and respect. You are two of the most honorable men I've ever met and I respect both of you highly."

"The feeling is mutual," Thunder said.

Sergeant Havoc shifted uncomfortably. "I like you guys too. You're not very military, but we can't all be perfect." He cracked a smile for the first time in hours.

"Here they come," Thunder declared, gazing down the corridor.

Twelve lizard-men marched up to the cell and posted themselves outside, their pikes leveled.

"Are you ready for round two?" the head of the detail inquired, producing a key from his left pants pocket.

"What's it going to be this time?" Sergeant Havoc inquired. "Gladiators? Wild beasts? Scuzzy mutants like you?"

The head of the detail grinned, opening the cell door. "I don't want to spoil the surprise. Reptilian has a treat in store for you."

"Do we get to fight Reptilian?" Havoc asked hopefully.

The lizard-man motioned for them to exit the cell. "No," he replied. "Reptilian does not need to prove himself in petty combat. This time you will face another of the Arena favorites."

"I hope the fans won't be disappointed when we win," Havoc declared.

"Dream on, human," the lizard-man stated. He waved them along the corridor.

The three men walked toward a wide door at the end of the hall.

"I lost a bet on your first bout," the Reptiloid remarked as the lizard-men tramped after the trio. "I won't lose on this one."

"Care to make a bet?" Havoc asked.

The Reptiloid laughed.

Boone, Havoc, and Thunder halted six feet from the door. Four of the lizard-man walked around them and unfastened a pair of metal bolts, then shoved the door open. The ominous glare of the Arena spilled into the corridor.

Sergeant Havoc squinted as he stepped outside. "Here we go again," he muttered.

Boone and Thunder advanced slowly. The door closed to their rear.

A ripple of applause stirred the audience as the Force members appeared.

"Sounds like we've got some fans," Havoc remarked stiffly.

"Greetings!" boomed a voice above them.

They turned and gazed upward.

Reptilian stood on the royal platform, a mocking smile upturning his lips.

"Where's Blade?" Boone asked anxiously. "I don't see Blade."

"He is not up there," Thunder confirmed.

"Hey, ugly!" Sergeant Havoc shouted. "Where's Blade?"

Reptilian placed his hands on his hips and glowered at the noncom. "Your overrated leader could not stand the sight of blood. He is sulking in his cell until the games are concluded."

Boone leaned toward Havoc. "He's not telling the truth."

"Don't you think I know it?" Sergeant Havoc responded.

Reptilian indicated the stands with a sweep of his left arm. "We trust you will be as entertaining as you were previously. I have arranged a suitable challenge to test your skills and courage."

"Let me guess!" Havoc baited the mutant. "We fight your mother!"

Reptilian's blue eyes became slits of wrath. "Your insolence will cost you, human. It will cost you dearly."

"Promises! Promises!" Havoc retorted.

"Let us see if you are so arrogant after you meet your adversary!" Reptilian declared. He gestured with his right arm.

A door to the right of the trio opened.

"You two stay behind me," Sergeant Havoc advised the frontiersman and the Flathead.

"We can take care of ourselves," Boone said.

"I'm the martial-arts ace here, not you," Havoc reminded him. "Let me take on whatever it is. You can be my backup."

"We're a unit, a team," Boone stated. "We'll take on whatever it is together."

A bulky figure stomped into the Arena.

"Good Lord!" Boone exclaimed.

"What is it?" Thunder inquired.

"I don't know," Sergeant Havoc said, "but I don't like it."

Their foe was a repulsive monstrosity displaying a variety of hybrid traits. It was essentially humanoid, with two legs and two arms. But what legs and arms! The limbs on the creature were as thick as the trunk of a towering tree, rippling with muscles and power. Its squat body was clothed in a tattered deer hide from its broad shoulders to its wide hips. A brown leather cord girded the garment at the waist. Its legs and feet were naked. The facial features were particularly arresting: a low, sloping forehead under a shaggy mane of black hair; two dark eyes under bushy brows; prominent cheeks and extremely bulbous lips; a square chin; and a pair of pointed ears.

"I've never seen anything like it!" Boone said.

"Reminds me of a blind date I had once," Sergeant Havoc quipped.

"It doesn't have a weapon," Thunder noted.

"It doesn't need one," Boone said.

The creature shifted to face them.

"Gentlemen!" Reptilian yelled down. "I would like to introduce you to Narg."

Havoc glanced up. "Great name! What'd you do? Pick the letters out of a hat?"

"Did you expect us to use mundane human names?" Reptilian retorted.

"Reptilian sounds mundane to me!" Havoc said, ridiculing the mutant leader.

"Reptilian is not my given name," the Reptiloid declared. "I selected it because of the fear the name instills. It is my title. My given name, the name my parents bestowed upon me, is Sauga. We are in the process of developing an official Reptiloid language. One day, our language will supplant English, Spanish, and every other human tongue. Wait and see."

"You mean I'll get to live that long?" Havoc taunted.

Reptilian smirked. "You should be so fortunate!" He stared at the creature. "Narg! Kill!"

The hybrid shuffled toward them as a man in black shut the door.

"Let me take him," Havoc said. Before the others could object, he dashed forward.

"Havoc! Wait!" Boone cried.

Sergeant Havoc was not in any mood to wait. Here was a golden opportunity to vent his accumulated anger, his seething resentment. He reached full speed, his eyes on the creature, amazed the thing wasn't making a move to defend itself.

Narg plodded toward the humans, seemingly oblivious to any danger they might pose.

Havoc grinned in expectation of an easy victory. He would show Reptilian!

"Havoc!" Boone shouted.

Sergeant Havoc came within ten feet of the hybrid and tensed his leg muscles. Eight feet. Six feet. He uttered a piercing kiai and launched himself into the air, performing a flawless Yoko-tobi-geri, a flying side kick, his right foot extended, his left tucked under his crotch. The maneuver, delivered by a master, could kill.

Havoc was such a master.

Narg was wrenched to the left by the impact as the heel of the noncom's combat boot slammed into his left cheek.

Havoc, expecting the creature to be rendered unconscious, suffered a rude awakening. His left boot glanced off Narg's cheek and he alighted in the cat stance three feet to the right of the hybrid.

Narg growled, revealing sawlike teeth.

Confounded by his failure, Havoc gaped at the creature's cheek, at the split skin and the flowing blood. Was that all? His best shot, and all he had accomplished was to inflict a minor cut?

Snarling, Narg suddenly whipped his right arm outward, striking with astonishing swiftness for one so heavy, his knuckles catching the noncom on the chin and sending Havoc catapulting backwards to sprawl in the dust.

"Kill him!" Reptilian goaded from the platform.

Havoc was on his stomach, motionless.

Narg took a step toward the human. His dull mind was slow to register the sensation of hands encircling his ankles from the rear. He felt those hands tugging on his legs, and he dimly realized the other two humans had attacked him from behind.

"Now!" Boone yelled, and strained his shoulder muscles to the utmost, his fingers locked on the creature's right ankle.

Thunder, applying his arms to the same task on the left ankle, grunted and heaved.

Together they succeeded where Havoc had not.

Narg voiced a rumbling growl as he abruply pitched onto his face. He placed his palms on the dirt and tried to rise.

Boone leaped onto the creature's back and wrapped his left arm around Narg's squat neck. He squeezed, hoping to choke the hybrid to death.

To Narg, the assault was scarcely worth noticing, the feeble attempt of a human flea to do him harm. He simply stood with the human clinging to his back, then unexpectedly bent forward at the waist.

Boone, unable to keep his grip, flew over the creature's head and smacked onto the ground. Intense pain lanced his left shoulder as he struck. He rolled and rose to his knees, clutching his injured shoulder.

Narg, like a tireless engine of destruction, closed in.

"Ho!" Thunder shouted, waving his arms to attract the creature. "Take me!"

Narg hesitated, distracted by the commotion.

"Take me!" Thunder repeated, backing away.

The Reptiloids and humans in the stands were cheering Narg on, certain their favorite could slay the outsiders.

"Me!" Thunder bellowed at the top of his lungs to make himself heard above the audience. "Me!"

Narg pivoted and lumbered after the Indian. He would finish off the others in a bit. First he must attend to the noisy one.

Thunder backpedaled to put more distance between the creature and his friends. He covered 15 yards and stopped, squatting on his haunches.

Narg shambled after the Indian, eager to end the battle and return to his peaceful cell where no one tried to hurt him and he was fed regularly. He disliked the bright lights of the Arena, the tumult and the violence.

"Ho!" Thunder called. "Come to me, demon!"

Narg was within eight feet of the human when his brain belatedly noted several strange details. Why wasn't the Indian running? Why was he crouched there, waiting to be caught? Why were his hands playing in the dirt? None of this behavior made any sense. Narg was accustomed to humans who fled, or else they fought with the desperation of the soldier with the fancy feet. They never just sat there, playing in the dirt. He halted.

Thunder's eyes narrowed. "Come to me, demon!"

Narg hesitated, confused.

"Are you afraid of me, demon?" Thunder asked. "Do you fear me because the Spirit-In-All-Things is in me?"

Narg had never been afraid in his life, but he did not like being made fun of, and he suspected this Indian was mocking him. Doing what all humans invariably did to him. His years in the wilderness of central Oregon had taught him to mistrust all humans. They either wanted to harm him or poke fun at him. Only the Reptiloids had treated him differently, had treated him with respect. A Hunter Squad had found him, had downed him after using seven darts. When he had awakened, Reptilian had been at his side. The Reptiloid leader had assured him that he had found a home at last. He was a mutant, like the Reptiloids. He was welcome to live with them, to be treated as an equal. All Reptilian had wanted was one service: Narg was to go to the Arena every so often and punish the bad humans Reptilian had captured.

And now this bad human was making fun of him!

"Come, demon!" Thunder said again. "Come to me!"

Narg lumbered forward. He saw the Indian smile. How could the Indian be so happy when he was about to die? He also saw the Indian's hands in the dirt, and he was watching those hands when they swept up, when they flung dirt directly into his eyes. Annoyed, he stopped and wiped at his eyes. They were blurry, filled with tears, and stinging terribly. He did not bother to hurry. The Indian, after all, could not harm him. He was Narg, the indistructible.

Or so he had been told by Reptilian.

Narg could feel the tiny grains of dirt smarting his eyes, and then he felt something else, something very odd.

Someone was fiddling with the leather cord about his waist.

Why would anyone do that?

Narg dabbed at his eyes, the tears dissipating, his vision clearing. He noticed the Indian was gone, then glanced down at his waist.

His belt was gone too!

Perplexed, Narg looked up. Why would anyone take his cord? He liked that sturdy cord, had worn it for years. Who could have taken it? The Indian?

A length of cord dropped over his head from the rear and wrapped itself around his neck.

What was this? Narg reached up, feeling the cord constricting tightly and biting into his skin. He tried to slip the fingers of his right hand under the cord, but his fingers were too stubby, the cord too taut. He became aware of someone standing behind him, not touching him, just standing there, and he put two and two together and perceived the Indian was trying to strangle him.

How interesting.

No one had ever tried this before.

Narg lashed his elbows backwards. The Indian, somehow, avoided the blows.

This was a tricky Indian!

With the cord sinking deeper and deeper into his neck, Narg

scratched his chin and worked on a plan. He needed to be as tricky as the Indian. An idea occurred to him and he smiled. He reached behind his head and gripped the cord.

The Indian pulled harder.

Narg jerked on the cord again and again, but his mighty sinews were unable to dislodge the Indian. He released the cord and dropped his arms, stumped.

What next?

He remembered the one on his back, the one he had tossed to the ground, and he immediately doubled over, hoping to duplicate the results. The Indian stumbled into his backside, and he swept his arms behind him and snatched at the Indian's legs. His left hand seized a handful of material, but the Indian pulled free before he could obtain a firmer grip.

Meanwhile, the cord was squeezing ever tighter and tighter.

Narg was becoming concerned. There was a pain in his throat, and he was finding it difficult to breathe. He glanced up at the royal platform and spotted Reptilian, his only true friend. Smiling, he indicated the cord encircling his neck and beckoned for Reptilian to come to his assistance.

Incredibly, Reptilian laughed.

Reptilian laughed?

Narg's forehead furrowed as he gazed at the Reptiloid leader. Why was Reptilian laughing? Why didn't Reptilian help him? Was Reptilian making fun of him like all the others? His mind balked at the thought. There was one way to find out.

Ask Reptilian.

With single-minded determination, Narg walked toward the wall below the royal platform. He could feel the Indian yanking on the cord, and he ignored this trivial distraction, concentrating on Reptilian. A look of astonishment flickered over the Retiloid's features, to be replaced by unbridled fury.

Why was Reptilian so mad?

Narg came within ten feet of the wall and halted. The cord around his neck had gone slack. He saw Reptilian rise and speak to one of the guards, and the guard handed over his pike. "Reptilian!" Narg called. "Why did you laugh?"

Reptilian moved to the rim of the platform, the pike in his right hand. "Why did I what?" he snapped.

The crowd was silent, collectively puzzled by Narg's peculiar behavior.

"Why did you laugh at me?" Narg asked.

"Why haven't you killed them?" Reptilian rejoined. He scowled and shook his head. "I am very disappointed in you."

"You laughed at me," Narg persisted, his mind focused on the single issue to the exclusion of all else.

Reptilian sneered. "Of course I laughed at you, you moron! Did you really believe I would come into the Arena to help you?"

"Why not help me?" Narg queried, flustered.

"You really are pathetic, do you know that?" Reptilian said derisively. "You have the intelligence of a turnip! I supply you with a place to live and I ensure you receive all the food you need. Why? Because I want you to do me a teensy-weensy favor. All you have to do is punish the bad people in the Arena when I tell you to. But do you obey me? No. I'm beginning to think I'm wasting my time with you. Why should I go to so much trouble if you won't do as you're told?"

"I'm tired of fighting all the time," Narg said. "I don't want to hurt people. I want to be happy."

"Be dead," Reptilian declared, and hurled the pike.

Narg saw the pike arcing toward him, and had his reflexes been commensurate with his awesome brawn he might have evaded the gleaming death. As it was, the pike struck him in the center of the forehead and burst out the rear of his cranium. He tottered for a moment, confounded by the tremendous headache he was suddenly experiencing, and then toppled over.

Reptilian gazed at the lifeless hulk for a moment. "Imbecile!" he said irately, and then shifted his attention to the Force members.

Thunder was ten feet from Narg's corpse, looking at the body with a sad expression. Boone was rising to his feet, rubbing his left shoulder. Sergeant Havoc was on his hands and knees, his head hung low, not yet in full possession of his faculties.

"I am through toying with you!" Reptilian shouted. "You have won your second bout by default. But there will not be any rest this time. You will face your next opponents now." He paused, grinning gleefully. "Are you ready to die?"

And from across the Arena a deep voice responded to the question, a voice with a menacing edge. "Are you?"

Reptilian swiveled in the direction of the voice, his eyes

widening as he beheld the giant human in the black leather vest and the fatigue pants. It couldn't be! He was supposed to be in his cell! But there he stood, next to an open door in the far wall, armed to the teeth, a large machine gun cradled in his arms.

"Blade!" Reptilian hissed.

Blade leveled the M-60 and raked the stands with his flinty gaze, finally focusing on Reptilian. The corners of his mouth curled upwards as he spoke. "Dying time is here."

CHAPTER NINETEEN

For ten seconds the Arena was perfectly still. Reptilian glared his hatred at the Warrior. The human section of the audience didn't know what to make of the giant's abrupt appearance. The Reptiloids were disconcerted, recognizing the threat the armed human posed and waiting for their leader to command them to action, to give the word.

He did.

"Kill him!" Reptilian bellowed.

A lizard-man on the wall above the Warrior lifted his pike overhead.

"Look out!" Boone shouted.

Blade was already in motion, spinning and tilting the M60's barrel upward at the Reptiloids in the stands. He squeezed the trigger and held it down, the big machine gun bucking and blasting with indiscriminate abandon.

Seated in the open, yards from the nearest exits, the vast majority unarmed, the Reptiloids were the proverbial sitting ducks. Some of the lizard-men attempted to let fly with their pikes, but they were cut down before they could complete the throw. Those in the stands were shown no mercy. The rain of slugs tore their bodies apart, bursting a chest here, a neck there, downing them in droves.

"Get that son of a bitch!" Reptilian shrieked, gesturing at his personal guard.

The guards started to head around the Arena, using an aisle near the wall. They managed less than ten yards.

"Not so fast, you pansies!" said a husky voice above and behind them.

Reptilian and the guards spun.

He was standing nonchalantly near the blue door, the door to the corridor connecting the royal platform to the stairwell, grinning and wagging the barrel of an M-16 toward the guards. His chest fur was caked with dried blood, he wore a camouflage

backpack, and a web belt containing spare clips encircled his waist.
"Going somewhere?" he asked sarcastically.

"Grizzly!" Reptilian yelled angrily. "You're a traitor to your
own kind!"

"Sticks and stones," Grizzly quipped, then crouched and fired.

"Get him!" Reptilian directed his personal guard, and they
sprinted toward Grizzly, never considering for a moment the
futility of pitting their pikes against an automatic rifle.

Reptilian was perched on the lip of the wall. He saw his guards
falling before Grizzly's withering fire, and he saw Blade drilling
the Reptiloids in the stands with the M60, and he knew he was in
trouble. Still, his subjects overwhelmingly outnumbered the
accursed giant and the bear-man, and sooner or later one of them
would cast a pike and end the fray. There was no way two
assassins could hold all of the Reptiloids at bay.

On the far side of the Arena dozens of Reptiloids were
swarming over the wall, bearing down on Blade. He was forced to
back up as he tried to prevent any of the lizard-men from getting
within pike range.

Grizzly had killed over a dozen of Reptilian's personal guard,
and still they came on. His back was to the blue door, the M-16
chattering.

Reptilian smiled.

Any moment now and it would all be over.

That was when a new element entered the battle. Athena
Morris raced into the Arena through the door in the far wall, her
arms laden with weapons and ammunition. She was heading in
the direction of Boone, Thunder, and Sergeant Havoc.

Reptilian leaned forward, his lips compressing. Blade must have
had all of this planned! While the giant kept his subjects in the
stands busy, and Grizzly did likewise with the royal guard, the
woman was going to carry weapons to their companions. Once
Boone, Thunder, and Havoc were armed, the Force stood an
excellent chance of defeating the Reptiloids.

No!

He couldn't allow that to happen!

The woman must not reach the men in the Arena!

Reptilian cast a hasty glance over his right shoulder, astounded
to discover Grizzly had discarded the M-16 and waded into the
elite guard wielding some sort of long claws. Grizzly was slashing

furiously, ducking and weaving to avoid the pikes, a smile on his face, as if he was thoroughly enjoying himself.

Athena was a third of the distance toward the three others.

Pandemonium reigned in the stands. The humans in the upper tiers were fleeing in stark panic out the exits, screaming and pushing and shoving in their eagerness to escape the Arena. Many of the Reptiloids, especially the females and the young ones, were also running away, contending with the humans to be the first to safety. Most of the male Reptiloids were converging on the Arena floor.

Reptilian leaped over the edge of the wall and dropped ten feet to the packed earth. He landed lightly and instantly took off toward Athena Morris. If you want something done right, he mentally observed, you must do it yourself! The woman must not reach her three male comrades, and he was the only one in a position to do anything about stopping her. And stop her he would!

Thunder and Boone had joined Sergeant Havoc and assisted the noncom in rising. They saw Athena running their way and moved to meet her halfway.

Reptilian, 15 yards behind the trio, poured on the speed. He covered ten yards and was rapidly gaining ground when he suddenly drew up short.

What was this?

Blade had inexplicably turned and was jogging after Athena.

Dozens upon dozens of Reptiloids were coming over the wall in pursuit.

Reptilian's forehead creased in confusion. What was Blade up to now? He perceived Blade would reach Athena and the others far ahead of his subjects. Was the Force planning to make a last stand in the center of the Arena? Or did Blade have an ulterior motive? Reptilian looked back at the royal platform.

A mad whirl of arms, legs, pikes and claws denoted the savage fight still raging.

Reptilian stared at Blade again, puzzled. A striking incongruity occurred to him: Why didn't Grizzly shoot when he'd had the chance? Grizzly could have shot him at any time up on the platform, but didn't. Why?

Athena Morris reached Boone, Thunder, and Havoc and began dispensing hardware.

Reptilian whirled and raced for the wall, angling to the right of the royal platform, heading for the door through which Narg had entered the Arena. The door was closed, but he was certain someone would be inside and could open it for him.

Blade spotted the Reptiloid leader and increased his pace. He glanced at his watch as he approached his colleagues.

Athena had handed out the weapons. Boone had his Hombres strapped around his waist. Thunder and Sergeant Havoc held M-16's and were checking the magazines.

"Havoc!" Blade shouted as he pounded up to them. "Take this!"

Sergeant Havoc was accustomed to taking orders. After years of military life, he was conditioned to obey an order instantly. He promply gave his M-16 to Thunder and took the M60 with no questions asked.

"I'm going after Reptilian," Blade said. "I want you to take care of the Reptiloids. Don't leave one alive." He paused. "And remember, we have seventeen minutes until detonation. When those charges go, the whole Imperium will come crashing down."

"Charges?" Boone repeated.

But Blade was gone, dashing across the Arena toward Reptilian. He saw the Reptiloid leader thumping on one of the Arena doors, apparently in an effort to have one of the lizard-men open the door from the inside. Blade gritted his teeth and ran all out. He was going to put an end to Reptilian's insanity or perish!

Reptilian was drumming on the door with both fists and yelling for someone to open it.

Blade's eyes flashed as he neared the mutant. He still had a dozen yards to cover. If the door wasn't opened, he would . . .

The door started to open.

Damn!

Blade ate up the distance with his lengthy strides. The door, much to Reptilian's annoyance, was opening very slowly. The lizard-man impatiently grabbed the outer edge and jerked the door outward.

Blade had ten yards to go.

Eight yards.

Prine appeared in the doorway, speaking to Reptilian. He glanced past the Reptiloid leader and pointed.

Six yards.

Reptilian rotated, his features distorted by rage. "Kill him! Kill him!" he thundered.

Prine was armed with a cudgel. He charged toward the Warrior, lifting the club.

Blade was in no mood to trifle with the Indoctrinator. He drew his Bowies as he ran, and when he came abreast of Prine he ducked to the right, avoiding the downward sweep of the cudgel, then moved in close. His left arm was a blur as he slit Prine's throat, and a fraction of a second later his right Bowie rammed into the Indoctrinator's stomach and twisted.

Prine released the cudgel, screeched, and clutched at his neck.

Blade yanked his right Bowie out and pivoted to face the door.

Reptilian had taken a step into the corridor beyond, wrongly assuming Prine would delay Blade long enough to permit him to escape. He froze as Prine lurched and sank to the ground, blood spraying from the Indoctrinator's severed throat and ruptured abdomen. A strategic withdrawal was now out of the question. Reptilian turned, smiling. Here was the human who presumed to challenge his authority! He would show the interloper the reason he was feared far and wide! He would show the fool the folly of his audacity!

Blade crouched, his bloody knives held close to his waist. "I was hoping you would stand and fight!"

Reptilian gazed over Blade's head at the carnage in the Arena. Piles of Reptiloid dead littered the earth, yet the Reptiloids continued to press their attack on the Force members. "Your people will soon be defeated!" he yelled to make himself heard.

Blade risked a look-see.

Sergeant Havoc was a few yards in front of the others, bearing the brunt of the Reptiloid charge. He swept the M60 with devastating effect, mowing the lizard-men down in rows. Thunder, Boone, and Athena were providing covering fire, guaranteeing none of the Reptiloids could outflank Havoc.

Blade stared at Reptilian and smirked. "You've got it backwards! Today is the day the New Order comes to an end!"

"Idiot!" Reptilian snapped. "Killing me will not destroy the New Order!"

"Let's find out," Blade proposed, taking a step nearer.

Reptilian's right hand vanished behind his back, disappearing in the folds of his cape.

Blade paused, unsure of what Reptilian was hiding under the red cape. It could be a gun.

Reptilian smirked, his right arm partially emerging. "What's the matter? Afraid?"

"I just don't like surprises," Blade responded. "What's under that cape?"

"Come closer and find out!" Reptilian suggested spitefully.

Blade's eyes narrowed. "You're bluffing! You don't have anything in your hand!"

"Come and see for yourself!" Reptilian baited him.

Blade cautiously circled to the left, hoping to glimpse the object. It could be a gun, but if it was a firearm, then why didn't Reptilian use it?

Reptilian turned, keeping his back hidden from view. "Why don't you leave while you have the chance?"

"I'm not leaving until you're dead!" Blade replied.

"You will be here forever!" Reptilian stated.

Blade took another stride. "I still say you're bluffing!"

Blade decided to call the lizard-man's bluff. He knew the Reptiloids did not issue firearms as standard ordnance. The sentries on the surface, those assigned to posts ringing the city, carried guns. But in the Imperium, pikes were the rule. Since Reptilian did not have a pike, the mutant must be unarmed. Such was the conclusion Blade reached, and he acted on his determination by springing at the Reptiloid leader.

Reptilian brought his right hand from under the cape and hurled an object at Blade's face.

Blade dodged, recognizing the walkie-talkie as it flew past his eyes. He vaulted forward, his arms outstretched.

Reptilian threw himself backwards, the tips of the Bowies missing his chest by a hair. He darted to the left, into the Arena.

Blade was not about to give the Reptiloid leader a moment's respite. He went after Reptilian, expecting the mutant to wheel and confront him.

Reptilian wasn't about to stop. He sprinted toward Narg's body, desperation lending wings to his feet.

Blade slowly slightly, mystified. He couldn't understand what Reptilian hoped to achieve by . . .

The pike!

Reptilian was going for the pike imbedded in the creature's

head!

Blade quickened his pace, knowing he would be at a severe disadvantage if the lizard-man got hold of the longer weapon.

Reptilian never looked back. He was nine feet ahead of the Warrior when he reached Narg's corpse, and he wrested the pike free with a powerful twist of his rippling shoulders. He twirled, bringing the pike up, and grinning in anticipation of his impending victory.

Blade stopped six feet from Reptilian, his arms out, the Bowies gleaming.

"How quickly the fortunes of war can turn!" Reptilian declared.

"Humans have a saying," Blade stated. "Don't count your chickens before they're hatched."

"And I have a saying," Reptilian retorted. "Death to all humans!" He hissed and jabbed the pike at Blade's knees.

Blade swatted the pike aside with a sweep of his right Bowie. He gave way, slowly backing up as the lizard-man pressed the onslaught.

Reptilian was extremely adept in the use of the pike. He had bested countless adversaries in pike combat during the years he was ascending to rulership of the Reptiloids. So he now employed every trick he knew, thrusts, counterthrusts, feints, frontal stabs, and side swings, and none of them worked. Blade parried every one, the pike and the Bowies clanging as they struck. Reptilian had never encountered a human endowed with such amazing strength and stamina, and his anger at being thwarted grew with each blocked strike. He considered throwing the pike, but what if he missed?

Blade was focusing all of his energy on simply staying alive. His arms were growing tired, and he hoped Reptilian would commit a fatal mistake before he did.

As they fought, as their weapons clashed again and again, Blade had continued to retreat, covering dozens of yards in the process.

Reptilian's shifty eyes spied a golden opportunity to end their contest. He renewed his assault, wanting to keep Blade's mind on their duel to the death, intending to prevent Blade from glancing to the rear.

Prine's blood-soaked body was five feet behind the Warrior.

Blade took one step backwards at a time. To rush would prove deadly. Concentrate! he commanded himself. Concentrate! He must keep his eyes on Reptilian's pike, his feet firmly on the ground. If he lapsed for a—

His left boot collided with something.

Blade tried to raise his boot and step over whatever was below him, but Reptilian suddenly drove the pike in a beeline for his heart. Forced to jerk his body to the rear to evade the pike point, he felt his boot slip on a wet substance. He tried to retain his balance, but the very next moment he was falling backwards, exposed and vulnerable.

Reptilian smirked as he surged forward, drawing the pike back to his ear and spearing the tip at the Warrior's midriff.

Blade landed hard on his shoulders and twisted onto his left side. The pike gouged a chunk of flesh from his stomach, but the wound was superficial. He ignored the pain and sliced his left Bowie across Reptilian's right leg.

Reptilian instinctively jumped back several feet, glancing down at his leg to assess the damage. His pants were slit and his skin was cut, but the leg was fully functional.

Blade used the reprieve to roll to the right and rise. He glimpsed Prine's corpse and realized he was covered with the Indoctrinator's blood.

"Damn you!" Reptilian fumed. "What does it take to finish you?"

"More than you've got," Blade said.

"Would you leave, right now, if I agreed to spare your life?" Reptilian unexpectedly asked.

"I'm not leaving until you're dead," Blade replied.

Reptilian scowled. "I will relish feasting on your flesh! I will boil your gonads in butter and eat them for my evening meal!"

"You're forgetting one thing," Blade said.

"What?"

"You have to win first," Blade declared.

"And win I shall!" Reptilian asserted.

"Not the way you fight," Blade said, deliberately insulting the Reptiloid. "If you're as good in bed as you are with that pike, the female Reptiloids must laugh themselves silly!"

"Why, you . . . !" Reptilian bristled, snarling and lunging, aiming the pike at the Warrior's face.

Which was what Blade wanted. He was not making any headway using the Bowies. Eventually the pike's greater reach would prevail. He needed to do something completely unforeseen, a move Reptilian would never anticipate.

Like so.

Blade snapped his head to the right as the pike lanced at his face. He abruptly released his Bowies and grabbed the pike shaft, clamping his fingers and pulling, adding his power to the momentum of Reptilian's thrust.

The lizard-man was unable to check his lunge. He stumbled forward, struggling to keep his grasp on the pike. The Warrior's left boot smacked into his shins, tripping him, and he fell to his hands and knees, the pike torn from his hands. He growled and stood.

Blade held the pike for a moment, letting Reptilian know he could use it if he wanted. Instead, he tossed the pike aside and crouched.

Reptilian seemed surprised by the move. "You're giving me a fair fight?"

Blade nodded. "One on one."

"You are dumber than Narg," Reptilian commented, and attacked.

Blade met the charge with a right to Reptilian's jaw. The mutant was staggered by the blow, and Blade followed through with a left to the gut and a right to the side of the Reptiloid's head.

Reptilian sagged, doubled over, gasping for air.

Blade formed a single fist from both hands and lifted them over his head.

Reptilian suddenly uncoiled, driving his right knee up and in, catching the Warrior in the groin.

Grunting, Blade bent over, his hands protecting his privates, racked by excruciating misery. He felt Reptilian's fingers lock onto his throat and he was rudely hauled erect.

Reptilian was smiling. "And so this farce ends!" he remarked.

"I agree," Blade said, wheezing, and swung his arms up and in, his rigid thumbs plunging into Reptilian's eyes. He pressed with all of his might.

Reptilian reflexively clawed at the Warrior's forearms, endeavoring to tear them from his eyes.

Blade held on, using his iron grip for leverage as he brought his right knee up, returning the favor, smashing his kneecap into the Reptiloid's crotch. Once. Twice. And twice more. With each blow Reptilian gurgled and trembled. "This is for Clayboss!" Blade commented, kneeing the mutant again. "And this is for Rivera," he added, sweeping his right knee up one more time.

Reptilian appeared to be having difficulty breathing. Spittle dripped from his lips.

"And this," Blade concluded, "is for Kraft!" His shoulder and arm muscles bunched, becoming rock hard, his triceps and biceps bulging. He fiercely snapped Reptilian's head to the right, then the left, and twisted.

There was a loud crack, a popping retort, and Reptilian slumped in the Warrior's grasp.

Blade let go and stood back.

Reptilian had a particularly stupid expression contorting his features, as if he couldn't believe his demise was possible. His knees buckled and he sagged to the ground.

Blade took a deep breath, regaining control of his emotions. He stared at the dead Reptiloid in grim satisfaction.

"Not bad for an amateur," remarked someone to his left. "I couldn't have done better myself."

Blade suddenly realized the Arena was quiet. He looked up.

Grizzly was on the Warrior's left, his fur splattered with fresh gore.

Boone, Thunder, Athena, and Sergeant Havoc stood seven feet away to the right.

"Where . . . ?" Blade began, surveying the stands and the Arena floor. Dead Reptiloids were literally everywhere.

"We killed as many as we could," Boone said. "The rest headed for the hills."

"It couldn't be helped," Athena chimed in. "We tried to get them all, like you wanted."

Sergeant Havoc was gazing at Reptilian. "My compliments, sir," he stated in his typically military fashion.

Blade remembered the explosive charges and checked his watch. "Let's move it, people!" he directed. "We have seven minutes to reach the surface. If we're in the Imperium when those charges detonate, we're as good as dead." He ran to his Bowies and scooped them up.

The Force members fell in behind him as he headed for the open door.

"What if there are humans still in the Imperium?" Boone mentioned. "Shouldn't we try to warn them?"

"There's no time," Blade replied over his left shoulder. "We'll barely have time to retrieve the radio from the armory."

"What about the Reptiloids who got away?" Boone queried. "Do we go after them?"

"No," Blade responded. "They're nothing without their leader. They won't give the Freedom Federation any more trouble."

He hoped.

EPILOGUE

He was seated at his desk in the command bunker when she entered.

"Grizzly said you wanted to see me," Athena said.

Blade looked up from the report he was writing on the Reptilian affair. "Yes. Have a seat."

Athena sat down in the chair in front of the desk.

"Are you all packed?" Blade asked.

"Athena nodded. "General Gallagher will be picking me up in an hour to take me back to LA."

Blade leaned back in his chair and folded his hands. "Grizzly tells me you did all right on this last mission."

"I don't think so," Athena said, frowning.

"Oh?"

. "I blew it too many times," Athena stated. "I wasn't as in control as I thought I would be."

"Staying calm in combat isn't easy," Blade remarked. "Like everything else in life, it takes practice."

"I don't see how you do it," Athena confessed.

Blade studied her thoughtfully. "Weren't you the one who wanted to do this on a regular basis? What happened to your ambition?"

"I don't know," Athena said reservedly. "I was shaken up out there. You may have been right."

Blade pursed his lips. "I don't know about that. You performed as well as any of the men."

Athena brightened. "You really think so?"

Blade nodded. "In fact, I have a proposition for you."

Athena grinned. "Aren't you married?"

Blade smiled and laid his hands on the desk. "You don't have to return to Los Angeles if you don't want to."

Stunned amazement was reflected in her countenance. "are you saying what I think you're saying?"

"If you still want to join the Force as a temporary member,"

Blade stated, "I'll go along with the idea."

Athena leaned forward, scrutinizing the Warrior intently. "What happened? Did Reptilian give you a concussion?"

"No," Blade replied, chuckling. "I'm serious."

"Wow!" was all Athena could think of to say.

"I need your answer now," Blade said.

"What's the rush?"

"We're leaving on another mission in three hours," Blade informed her. "I just got off the phone with General Gallagher."

"Three hours?" Athena repeated doubtfully. "So soon?"

"I'm afraid so," Blade said. "I haven't told the others yet. I know they like you, and they would be happy to have you stay. I figure I can give them some good news with the bad. So how about it? Will you sign on or not?"

Athena hesitated. Here was the realization of her dreams, the chance to write her own ticket. All she had to do was say yes.

"I'll understand if you decline," Blade commented. "This is a harzardous profession. In two missions we've lost four men. We're bound to lose more."

"What if I blow it again?" Athena inquired apprehensively. "I could endanger everyone else."

Blade shrugged. "We all run that risk."

"This situation reminds me of the motto my grandfather had," Athena said. "No pain, no gain."

"Does this mean you'll accept?" Blade asked.

"I must be out of my mind," Athena stated, her excitement rising, "but yes, I accept."

"Good," Blade said. "I'll let you break the good news to the others. Don't tell them about the new mission. I'll be over to the barracks in five minutes and fill them in."

Athena stood, beaming happily. "I wonder if I know what I've gotten myself into!"

"You're in an elite military unit," Blade observed. "The key word is military. We may not go strictly by the book, but there are rules and regulations you'll be expected to follow, just like the others."

"Military decorum and all that. Is that what you mean, Big Guy?" Athena inquired.

"I suppose so," Blade said. "And stop calling me Big Guy."

"We could have a problem with military decorum," Athena mentioned.

"What kind of problem?"

"What am I going to do on laundry days?" Athena queried solemnly. "Should I hang my undies on the line with the rest of my uniform, or would General Gallagher have a fit?"

Blade laughed and waved her toward the door. "Go break the good news to the others. I have a report to complete."

Athena scooted to the doorway, then paused. "Blade?"

The Warrior looked over at her. "What?"

"From the bottom of my heart," Athena said sincerely. "Thanks."

"You've earned it," Blade assured her.

"If you say so," Athena said. "But thanks just the same." She paused and laughed. "You Big Lug."

HARD RIDING WESTERN ADVENTURE FROM LEISURE BOOKS

by Nelson Nye. Tens of millions of Nelson Nye titles in print! One of his most unusual and action-packed Western tales!

_____2431-4 $2.50 US/$3.25 CAN

GUNBLAZE by Lee Bishop. A returning Confederate veteran takes on an army of renegades to carve out a new life for himself in the west.

_____2410-1 $2.50 US/$3.25 CAN

SUNDANCE: TRAIL DRIVE by Peter McCurtin. He's half-Indian, half-white and all-trouble. Blazing Western action.

_____2384-9 $2.50 US/$2.95 CAN

AFTER THE NUCLEAR WAR WAS OVER — THE REAL KILLING BEGAN

They called him Phoenix because he rose from the ashes of destruction, driven by hatred, and thirsting for revenge. Battling nature gone insane and men driven mad by total devastation, he forged his way across a nightmare landscape.

The action/adventure series that's hotter than a thermonuclear explosion, by

DAVID ALEXANDER

_____2462-4 #1: DARK MESSIAH
$2.95 US/$3.75 CAN

_____2517-5 #2: GROUND ZERO
$2.95 US/$3.75 CAN

_____2571-X #3: DEATH QUEST
$2.95US/$3.75 CAN